# THE DECEMBER POSTCARDS

by Alayne Smith

Ellard
publishing

Lawrenceville, GA

© 2024, Alayne Smith
All rights reserved.

**The December Postcards**

Ellard
publishing

Published by Ellard Publishing
Lawrenceville, GA

ISBN 978-1-7366448-5-0 paperback
ISBN 978-1-7366448-6-7 e-book

Library of Congress Control Number: 2024915658

All rights reserved. For the personal use of the purchaser only. This book may not be reproduced in whole or in part, without written permission from the author. Nor may any part of this book be reproduced, stored in a retrieval system, or transmitted in any form or by any means whatsoever, electronic, mechanical, copying, recording, scanning or otherwise.

This is a work of fiction. Unless otherwise indicated, all characters are the product of the author's imagination. Any resemblance to actual persons, living or dead, is purely coincidental.

The John F. Kennedy Speech on the Cuban Missile Crisis was made from the Oval Office in the West Wing of the White House on October 22, 1962. Source: https://www.jfklibrary.org/learn/about-jfk/historic-speeches/address-during-the-cuban-missile-crisis, from the John F. Kennedy Presidential Library and Museum website, accessed Aug. 14, 2024.

The hymn texts that appear in this book are taken from *The United Methodist Hymnal: Book of United Methodist Worship*, published by The United Methodist Publishing House, Nashville, TN, 1989.

Author Website: https://alaynesmith.com

# Chapter One
*Friday, October 12, 1962*

Ree leans her body into the October wind as she turns the corner onto Crogan Street where the hotel lords over surrounding stores. If she weren't in such a hurry, she might notice that all the stores sport smiling pumpkins with misshapen square teeth. Carved by students from the elementary school that sits at the top of the hill, the pumpkins add to orange, yellow, and white mums lining the street. Ree loves Lawrenceville. She loves that spooky, mystical Halloween is coming to Lawrenceville, Georgia, with or without Ree's permission.

Short for Reeda, Ree means "favored, popular, loved." *Yeah, right.* Right now, she feels harried, stressed, and late. She is rushing home from the *Lawrenceville News-Herald* to cook dinner for her father, James, and her thirteen-year-old daughter, Virginia. *Good grief, what a week. It is going to be tuna casserole again this Friday.*

Home is a two-story wooden house, the once-brilliant white paint on the home's exterior now almost nonexistent. In town, the house is known as the Alfus Martin House, named after James' grandfather. He built the house ages ago on Clayton Street where it sits across from the courthouse alongside the Feely House.

Ree admits it's an eyesore. Maybe one day, she and her father will restore it. She shudders. That's an iffy thought. Her father, James Martin, has not been the same since his wife, Mildred, was murdered. Mildred had been the spark that kept James and Ree and half the town of Lawrenceville going.

Besides keeping the books at James' law office, Mildred had been active in the Lawrenceville Garden Club and a member of both the canasta club and the bridge club. She volunteered at the public library and was a docent at the famous Feely House next door.

And she was Ree's mother.

A mother who nurtured. A mother who let Ree pick out her own clothes. A mother who listened to her daughter's childhood woes while teaching her to be responsible and loyal and to love deeply.

Ree was just twelve when her mother was murdered. Her father, James, found Mildred's body in the library of the Feely house. When she had not come home from volunteering by supper time, he had gone looking for his wife. This was highly unusual, as Mildred was usually home in time to have a cup of coffee and discuss the day with James before she made dinner for the family.

The cause of death had been a blow to the head. The sheriff found Uncle Richard's cane, the one with the solid silver grip, near her mother's body. It appeared to be the murder weapon.

Uncle Richard, her father's older brother, had been a professor of history at Emory at the time. It was rumored he never married because he, Richard, was in love with Mildred. But he could never have killed Mildred. Ree would never believe that.

The sheriff had arrested Richard, but before he could be arraigned, Richard somehow escaped from the Lawrenceville jail. He has not been seen or heard from since the escape decades ago.

Or has he?

Ree stomps her feet at the front door to remove the street's dirt from her shoes and yells as she enters, "Dad, Virginia… where are you?"

"Reeda, stop bellowing. I'm in the front parlor," says James.

Ree walks into the parlor that hasn't changed a bit since they lost Mildred. The velvet Art Deco sofa and high-backed floral chair were still impeccably arranged to face the fireplace, flanked by a wooden secretary and chair on the left and the door to the dining room on the right.

Virginia finds her father leaning over the coffee table looking at a series of postcards splayed across the table. The postcards have come from all over the world. James has received one every

## The December Postcards

December since the year after Mildred's death. The postcards are totally blank—no personal note and no indication of who they are from. Rather than talk about the postcards again, Ree kisses her father softly on the forehead.

"I'm starting dinner now, Dad."

"Okay, darling. Oh, and don't forget your Aunt Clarisse's funeral is this Thursday. First one of us Martins to be cremated. Don't understand that at all."

"It's on my calendar, Dad," she says as she walks toward the kitchen.

She finds Virginia working on something, probably homework, at the kitchen table. Ree's heart always seems to skip a beat when she looks at her indomitable daughter. Virginia has the makings of a real beauty, with huge blue eyes that don't miss much and a full mouth that breaks into a captivating smile at the slightest provocation. Virginia is totally unaware of her looks and that makes her more attractive.

Ree looks for herself in her daughter but finds her husband, Mason, instead. Mason and Ree had known each other all their lives, but the two moved in different circles. They had never paid attention to each other until their tenth-grade Spanish class, where they were known by the names Juan and Margarita. Juan fell in love with Margarita the first time she corrected his pronunciation.

# The December Postcards

After high school Mason joined the Army Air Corp and Ree went to the University of Georgia to get a journalism degree. Mason and Ree continued their relationship long distance. They married in 1945 but their life together had been short-lived. Mason was killed in September 1950 when General MacArthur led a surprise attack against North Korea, with an amphibious landing behind enemy lines.

Ree buried Mason, but to her, he is still here, with her. Not a day goes by that she doesn't ask Mason's advice or tell him what's happening here in Lawrenceville.

Ree is jerked back to reality when Virginia says, "Mom, Granddaddy is going through all those old postcards again. Why does he do that?"

"Remember, Daddy thinks they are from his brother, Richard. Richard was accused of your grandmother's death but ran away before he could be tried."

"That's some family mystery. I wish we could solve it for Granddaddy."

Ree pauses a moment and looks at her daughter, almost astonished at the thought.

*Well why not? Why don't I try to solve it? As if I don't have enough to do with taking care of these two and working at the* News-Herald. *But why not? At the very least, I can look at the newspaper articles from the time of the murder. Why have I never thought to do that? If I can find out who is sending the cards, maybe—just maybe—I can find out who killed Mother.*

"Now, Virginia, where is that can of tuna?"

Virginia sighs. "It's behind you on the counter, Mom. And the noodles are there, too."

"Oh, okay, okay. I'd lose my head, if it weren't for you. Now, while I get this casserole ready, tell me about your day."

Virginia perked up. "It was so much fun! We got to help the Chicken Coop kids carve pumpkins for Perry Street. Crogan Street is already lined with pumpkins from the third and fourth graders. Did you walk home that way? Did you see them?"

Ree smiles now as she always does when she hears the block building housing the first and second grades referred to as the Chicken Coop. "I am sorry. I did walk home that way but didn't notice. We're already decorating for Halloween?"

"Mom, Halloween is less than three weeks away. Of course, we're decorating."

"Good grief," says Ree as she slides the tuna casserole into the oven.

# DISCLAIMER

The information contained in this book and its components, is meant to serve as a comprehensive collection of strategies that the author of this book has done research about. Summaries, strategies, tips and tricks are only recommendations by the author, and reading this book will not guarantee that one's results will exactly mirror the author's results.

The author of this book has made all reasonable efforts to provide current and accurate information for the readers of this book. The author and its associates will not be held liable for any unintentional errors or omissions that may be found.

The material in the book may include information by third parties. Third party materials comprise of opinions expressed by their owners. As such, the author of this book does not assume responsibility or liability for any third party material or opinions.

The publication of third party material does not constitute the author's guarantee of any information, products, services, or opinions contained within third party material. Use of third party material does not guarantee that your results will mirror our results. Publication of such third party material is simply a recommendation and expression of the author's own opinion of that material.

Whether because of the progression of the Internet, or the unforeseen changes in company policy and editorial submission guidelines, what is stated as fact at the time of this writing may become outdated or inapplicable later.

This book is copyright ©2021 by **Thinknetic** with all rights reserved. It is illegal to redistribute, copy, or create derivative works from this book whole or in parts. No parts of this report may be reproduced or retransmitted in any forms whatsoever without the written expressed and signed permission from the author.

## Chapter Two
*Tuesday, October 16, 1962*

Ree parks her dented turquoise car in front of the Western Auto Store on Perry Street just as lawyer Harold Perry descends the stairs from his law office located above the store. Ree steps out of her car, notices him walking toward her, and yells, "I don't have time for you, Harold." She slams the car door behind her and walks down the street, leaving a resigned Harold behind her.

Miss Birdie, who works at Cato's next door, witnesses the whole scene and comes out of the store. Named appropriately, Miss Birdie is tall with pencil-thin legs and hair with swirls on top of her head in a manner that makes her head look like a bird's nest. Patting Harold on the arm, Miss Birdie says, "Now, Harold Perry, don't you let that Martin girl get you down. You are the best-looking and smartest unattached male in Lawrenceville. She's bound to notice you sooner or later."

"Thank you for your vote of confidence, Miss Birdie," says Harold.

Ree never looks back. She crosses Pike Street and walks into the *News-Herald* building. It's a second home to Ree. She's been working there in one form or another since she was in high school. Currently, Ree is a reporter, covering four to five stories a day for the weekly paper.

Walking into the foyer, Ree greets Miss Betty Holland who serves as receptionist and secretary for the paper. She greets customers from behind a long wooden counter that faces the front door. Miss Betty is wearing one of her many silk, tie-neck blouses today, the large bows tied with perfection. No bow is going to droop while Miss Betty is wearing it.

Miss Betty removes her cat eye glasses and asks, "Have you gone out on a date with that handsome Harold yet?"

Ree sighs, "No, Miss Betty. I have not." She wishes Miss Betty would mind her own business.

Hearing the conversation, Mary Burns, the bookkeeper, walks up and says "You are wasting time, girl. Someone else is going to grab him," says Miss Mary.

"Not you, too, Miss Mary."

Quickly changing the subject, Ree tells the ladies she will be working in the storage room if the manager, Mr. Monroe, needs her. She leaves the room before Betty and Mary can plan her wedding.

In the main newsroom, Ree turns left and heads into the storage room where back issues of the paper are stored. She is on a mission and does not want to be distracted by other staff members. Heavy metal shelves that cover two walls of the storage room hold the red, leather-bound books that contain copies of the *News-Herald* from 1898 to the present.

Ree chooses a volume that includes papers from October 1934 and sets it down on a wooden table with a scarred top and sagging middle. The table appears to be part of the original furnishings in the storeroom. Ree turns the pages of the bound book slowly until she finds the October 4 issue. On the front page, above the fold, she finds the article she's searching for.

*Prominent Citizen Finds Wife Dead in the Feely House*

**Local lawyer James Washington Martin found his wife, Mildred Louise Martin, dead in the library of the Feely House on the afternoon of October 3, 1934. Martin went in search of his wife when she had not returned by dinner time from the Feely House, where Mildred Martin is a volunteer docent.**

**Martin immediately called Sheriff Croft. After investigating the scene, the sheriff declared the death a homicide. Sheriff Croft stated, "It has to be a homicide. The deceased has an open wound on the top right of her head. A walking cane with blood on the ornate silver head was found at the scene of the crime."**

**The sheriff searched the property with his deputies for more than two hours after arriving**

> at the scene. Finding no further clues, Sheriff Croft released the body to Lawrenceville Coroner Thomas Jefferson Jones.
>
> Services will be held at the Lawrenceville Methodist Church on Sunday, October 7, at 2:00 p.m. and will be officiated by Reverend W. M. Ames.

Ree finishes the article and lowers her head to her arms crossed on the worn surface of the table. Seeing the story in print makes her heart ache. There's a physical pain in her chest. Sorrow and anger all balled up together. Anger because all these years later no one knows who killed her mother.

*A murderer is walking around out there. Have they killed before? Will they kill again? Will Ree be a threat if she gets involved?*

The sorrow never leaves.

Reading the article brings it all back—her father crying in the living room, the relatives who came to stay for days, weeks even, and the endless stream of caring Methodist ladies bringing their fried chicken, any number of casseroles made with onion soup dip, and love. They surrounded Ree and her family with such love and kindness, for which she was thankful. Most of all, Ree remembers her father crying.

Finally, Ree raises her head. She re-reads the sentence about Thomas Jefferson Jones and smiles. Thomas Jefferson, the coroner, is a distant relative of her husband, Mason. Not only is Thomas Jefferson Jones the coroner, he's the custodian at the courthouse as well. He has to be older than dirt, and, when you enter the courthouse, you are bound to see him with his ragged pinstripe overalls and starched-stiff white shirt. Ree smiles again thinking of Thomas Jefferson mopping the floors of the courthouse.

Funny thing about the custodian and coroner Thomas Jefferson, he's scared to death of dead bodies. When called to the scene of a death, he barely looks at the body before pronouncing it dead. One of these days he's going to make a mistake, and one of his bodies is going to get up and walk out of the morgue. Ree turns more pages and notices an unrelated article.

*Local Criminal Escapes During Al Capone Transfer*

**Billy Faucett from Snellville, Georgia, escaped from the Atlanta Penitentiary on October 1, 1934, during the transfer of Al Capone from the penitentiary to Alcatraz off the coast of California. Faucett was incarcerated in 1932 after being tried and found guilty of murdering local Snellville woman, Edna Jane Hixson.**

**It is believed Faucett is guilty of murdering five other local ladies during the early 1930s. Those murders are still unsolved. The murderer in these unsolved cases is referred to as "The Hammer" because blunt force trauma to the head is his mode of operation.**

**Al Capone, who smuggled and bootlegged liquor during Prohibition in the 1920s, was convicted of tax evasion in 1931. He spent three**

> years in the Atlanta Penitentiary before his transfer to Alcatraz Federal Penitentiary.
>
> Sheriff Croft assures the public Faucett will be caught and returned to the Atlanta Penitentiary before the week is out.

"Reeda, Betty said you are in here. Where are you?" The voice of her boss, Mr. Monroe, startles her.

"Back here, Mr. Monroe," she says.

Clyde Monroe, a journalism degree from the University of Georgia in hand, came to work at the *News-Herald* in the 1930s and never left. He married his high school sweetheart, Peggy Lockhart, and brought her with him to Lawrenceville. Mr. Monroe has two loves—Miss Peggy and the *News-Herald*.

Now general manager, Mr. Monroe had in his day been an outstanding reporter, one of the paper's best. Despite having polio as a child and walking with a limp, he covered any number of stories that made the news worldwide, like the Winecoff Hotel fire in 1946. It was the deadliest hotel fire in American history and killed 119 occupants of the Atlanta establishment that had been touted by its builders to be fireproof. He had been nominated for a Pulitzer Prize for that story.

Mr. Monroe walks to the back of the room where Ree sits at the table. Ree can hear his cane clicking on the wooden oak floor long before he reaches the table. She closes the binder, so Mr. Monroe can't see what she's researching.

Looking up just as Mr. Monroe approaches, Ree says, "Hi, Mr. Monroe. I'm doing a little research. Did you need me?"

"Yes. I need you to proof your aunt's obituary. But did you hear the news about Cuba?

"No. Bad news?"

"Yes, I'm afraid so. Russian missiles have been located in Cuba. Bad news for our country," says Mr. Monroe.

"Yes, it certainly is, but how do we know missiles are in Cuba?"

"Two days ago, one of our U-2 spy planes photographed nuclear missile sites being built there. President Kennedy warned Cuba about that very thing back in July. Seems there was evidence then of Soviet build-up in Cuba.

"This is scary. What happens now?"

"It's my understanding President Kennedy is meeting with his advisors. Who knows where this will lead. And, you're right, it is scary."

"You want me to look at Aunt Clarisse's obituary?" asks Ree

"Please. Clarisse Martin will haunt me from her grave if I print an error in the paper. See what you think." Mr. Monroe hands a sheet of paper to Ree.

> We are sad to announce the passing of Clarisse Lee Martin of Lawrenceville, Georgia. She died at age ninety-one on October 10, 1962. Clarisse passed away surrounded by her loved ones after a battle

with pneumonia. The funeral will be held at the Lawrenceville Methodist Church on Thursday, October 18, 1962 at 10:30 a.m.

Ree reads the notice then hands it back. "Not an error in sight, Mr. Monroe."

"Thank goodness. Are you still working on that story about the dedication of the bridge on 120 Highway to Marvin Allison?"

"Yes, sir. I'll give it to you after lunch."

"Okay, Reeda. I'll leave you to it."

Ree waits until the sound of the tapping cane fades away before opening the book again.

## Chapter Three
*Thursday, October 18, 1962*

"Good morning. You are listening to WLAW… the Law," shouts Johnny Day, morning deejay for the local radio station.

Ree opens one eye. *Oh, no. It can't be seven o'clock.*

"Here's a little tune to get you jumping and jiving, 'Green Onions.' Wake up, Lawrenceville."

Ree fumbles with the snooze button on the radio until there is quiet. She is sinking ever so slowly back into a world of fuzzy images and sweet contentment when thoughts fire through her brain like bullets.

*Aunt Clarisse's funeral is today. Is Dad's dress shirt ironed? What will Virginia wear? What will she wear?*

"And that's Booker T. and the MGs," shouts Johnny Day.

"Good grief," says Ree as she hits the power switch to turn Johnny Day off for good. Ree puts both feet on the floor. She feels around with one foot for her fuzzy bedroom shoes. Accomplishing that, she stands up, grabs her robe off the foot of the bed, and heads for the kitchen.

Ree smells the strong nutty-flavored coffee as she walks into the kitchen where James stands buttering his toast at the kitchen counter. Like the living room, this kitchen is still Mildred's room with its soft yellow walls, glossy white cabinets, and starched café curtains covering the bottom half of the windows that skirt the dining area in the spacious kitchen.

"Morning, Sug. Want some breakfast?" says James.

Ree is surprised to see James in the kitchen this morning. He is usually at Edge's for breakfast with his best friend, Gus.

"I'll take a piece of toast with my coffee. What's going on in the world today?"

"Soviet Foreign Minister Gromyko denies the Soviets have weapons in Cuba," says James.

"But we have photographs to prove they have missiles in Cuba," says Ree.

"Well, President Kennedy met with Gromyko. He told him the United States will not tolerate Soviet missiles in Cuba. The Soviet Union has been warned. We'll see what they do."

"It's a story to follow, Dad. Let me get breakfast in me, and I'll check on your shirts. We need to be at the church no later than 9:30."

## The December Postcards

\* \* \*

Walking around the corner to the Methodist Church, Ree looks up at the two square turrets with notched tops atop the church and wonders what the builder was thinking. *Maybe about medieval castles?*

On the sidewalk ahead, Ree notices Senator Scott and his mousy wife, Delia. My gosh, the man is pompous. He struts. He is quite the picture with his gray wool suit, solid red tie, and matching pocket square. His hair is slicked back with hair cream. Standing near him, Ree gets a faint whiff of a citrusy smell. The senator reminds Ree of a particular Bantam rooster that inhabits the courthouse square and crows to show his dominance over the other creatures.

The senator turns to say something to Delia. He sees James, Ree, and Virginia and stops in his tracks. He says, "We are so sorry for your loss, James. Aren't we Delia?" Delia takes a step back, but nods her head toward James.

Delia is a shy, awkward lady. She is taller than the senator and looks elegant in her black and white, full-shirted dress with its high stand-up collar and three-inch black stretch belt. Ree has seen that dress at Alford's, and it is waaay expensive. Even though she is taller than her husband, Delia seems to take up less space than the strutting senator.

James tips his hat and says, "Thank you for the sentiment, Senator Scott. You, too, Mrs. Scott. Thank you as well."

Delia nods and turns to follow the senator down the sidewalk.

James passes between the towering white columns and walks up the church steps, followed by Ree and Virginia. They move to join other family members on the porch. They will enter the right door to walk down the aisle en masse and sit on the front rows of the sanctuary.

Ree immediately spots Aunt Maude standing with two distinguished-looking men who might be Aunt Clarisse's former husbands. Ree and Virginia walk over to them. Before they can speak, they are directed to form a line to walk into the sanctuary, which they do to the strands of "Joyful, Joyful, We Adore Thee."

Aunt Clarisse's service is blessedly brief. Reverend Foster reads Aunt Clarisse's favorite Bible verse from 1 Corinthians, chapter 13, about love and talks about her aunt's many contributions to the community. The full choir is in attendance and sings "Morning Has Broken" flawlessly. The service ends with Amanda Martin, a cousin from Dahlonega, singing a beautiful rendition of "Amazing Grace."

As mourners leave the church, Glenda Stovall plays "Ave Maria" on the church organ. Ree sits quietly on the velvet-cushioned church pew as the last strands of organ music fade away. James and Virginia have already gone outside, but Ree thinks it feels right to just sit and think about her aunt. What a character she was. She married three times. If you believe the gossip, she had many loves beyond that.

Aunt Clarisse was what her Lawrenceville friends would call "stinking rich" with the monies passed down to her from her father, Lawrence Martin, and her grandfather, Alfus Martin. Clarisse had studied in Austria and lived in Paris for years, but she came home to Lawrenceville in her fifties. From the moment she returned, Lawrenceville was not the same.

Aunt Clarisse was a Republican in a bed of Democrats and used her money to put Republicans on the City Council and anywhere else she could stick them. She used her money to support the Methodist Church, too. Last year, after visiting the parsonage for some affair, she outfitted the parsonage living room with all new furniture from Home Furniture up on the square. Dad says she told him the furniture in the parsonage wasn't fit for her dog.

Ree smiles as she stands up to leave the church, thinking about Aunt Clarisse. She was one of a kind. Stepping out into the aisle, Ree sees Howard Perry walking toward her. She feels guilty about the way she treated him earlier but just as she opens her mouth to say so Harold cuts her off, "As I tried to tell you Tuesday, I am the executor of your Aunt Clarisse's will. She has left specific instructions on the dispersion of her ashes, and she has chosen you to disperse them."

Ree's jaw drops and she stares blankly at Harold. It's not only what he says, but the way he says it—icy cold. After a beat, she finds her words.

"But I don't understand. I'm to disperse her ashes? Why me?"

"Obviously, she saw something in you she liked. She once told me you had a good head on your shoulders," says Harold, handing Ree a set of papers.

Ree looks down at the papers in her hand. There seem to be rather lengthy instructions—a lot of verbiage for such a simple task. *Isn't spreading ashes supposed to be straightforward?* She begins to read.

First, Aunt Clarisse wants a portion of her ashes spread on Margaret Mitchell's grave, because she loved *Gone with the Wind*; it was her favorite book. Second, she wants ashes spread in the rose garden beside the Lawrenceville Methodist Church. *Enough.* Ree doesn't want to read further.

"Have you read this, Harold?" she says.

"I have."

"Isn't this illegal—what she's asking me to do?"

"I don't think so. But that's your problem," says Harold, turning to walk away.

"Harold," shouts Ree. "I'm sorry I was rude to…"

Harold stops and turns. "The trouble with you, Reeda, is that you think every man in Lawrenceville under the age of fifty wants to jump your bones. You have quite an elevated opinion of yourself." Harold stalks out of the sanctuary.

Ree enters the closest pew and plops herself down again.

*I have an elevated opinion of myself? That's ridiculous. And who would ever think Harold Perry could be so angry?*

After a moment, she reads the document in her hands. *My gosh, Aunt Clarisse. What were you thinking?*

No answer from Aunt Clarisse. Just the soft voices of people outside the church talking amongst themselves.

## Chapter Four
*Friday, October 19, 1962*

Ree begins her day by visiting Mason's grave. Kneeling in the brittle grass beside the grave, Ree tells her husband how well Virginia is doing at school and how happy she is. She mentions her dad and the postcards, too, and confesses she is looking into their mysterious origins and how they may relate to her mother's murder. Ree tells Mason she questions why she is even chasing the details so many years later. After a moment, she answers herself.

*To take that sad look off Dad's face. That's why.*

Leaving the historic cemetery, Ree decides to stop by for a visit with Sheriff Pitts. Driving to the square, she parks in front of Monfort Drugs. No sign of Harold on Perry Street.

*Why should she be looking for Harold anyway? He obviously wants nothing to do with her.*

Ree walks up the steps of the courthouse and into Sheriff Pitt's office. He is on the phone when she walks in but quickly finishes his call. Smiling at Ree, he says, "That's Miss Angie again. Someone is stealing apples from the trees in her backyard.

I don't understand people. Miss Angie will never eat all those apples. Why not put them in a basket on the sidewalk in front of her house with a "Free Apples" sign? Everyone would be happier, including my deputies. Now, what can I do for you, Miss Ree?"

Ree hesitates.

"It can't be that bad," says the sheriff. "Here, have a seat, and let's talk." He motions toward an empty chair.

"It's about my mother. I know you know the history. It bothers me that all these years later we don't have a solution. We don't know who murdered her. It's on my mind. Do you have a file on her? If you do, will you share it? I know it was over twenty years ago, but would you check?"

Sheriff Pitts walks to the file cabinet in the back of the room and returns with a worn folder. Mildred Martin's name is written on the bent tab.

"I am going to spare you the details from the medical examiner. Suffice it to say death was caused by a strike to the head. Let's see what else is in the file."

"There was a cane found, correct?" says Ree.

"Yes. It was found near your mother's body. It is described in the file as an Indian rosewood cane topped with a solid silver knob. It is unique because of the small, metal cane badges nailed into the wood—badges from India, Scotland, Wales. It is Richard's cane. Evidently your uncle was quite the traveler."

"Was it the murder weapon?"

"Yes. The wound on your mother's head matched the shape of the knob. The medical examiner identified matter found on the head of the cane as coming from your mother."

"And my Uncle Richard was arrested the next day?"

"Yes. The file indicates he was."

"But if he murdered my mother, why would he leave the cane? Everyone in town probably knew it was his."

"We will never know that answer, Reeda. By the way, your father has not heard from Richard, has he?"

Ree looks the sheriff straight in the eye before she answers, "No, he has not."

"I thought as much," says the sheriff.

"Is there anything else in the file?"

Sheriff Pitts digs around in the file and lifts out a form. "This report is in the file. It's a statement made by Senator Scott. He told the sheriff that he saw Richard's car in front of the Feely House the afternoon of the murder."

"That's news to me. It seems the cards were stacked against Uncle Richard, but I can't see the Uncle Richard I knew murdering anyone."

"Funny how these things turn out. I know it just about killed your dad. I hear they were close."

"We were all close to Uncle Richard, but he and Dad were extremely close." Ree stands up to leave. "Thank you, Sheriff Pitts, for sharing with me."

"Young lady, my advice is that you let this alone. We'll never know for sure who killed your mother."

"You are probably right," Ree says over her shoulder as she leaves the department.

* * *

Ree slowly walks down the street and sits in her car. She lays her head back on the worn, white leather of the seat and closes her eyes. She lets the memories come.

Ree is ten years old. As she walks home from school, a boy from her class—Terry something; Ree has forgotten his last name—shoves her to the sidewalk and spits toward her. "Why do you always have to know everything?" he says.

The boy turns and runs down the sidewalk straight into Uncle Richard. Ree remembers what happened next in vivid detail. Uncle Richard grabs Terry by the arm and drags him back to where she lay on the sidewalk. "Now, you tell me why you hurt my niece," he says in a booming voice.

Ree can see Terry is scared. *Not such a bully now.* Terry hangs his head and won't say a word.

"Maybe the sheriff can get you to talk," says Uncle Richard.

With his head still lowered, Terry says, "She knows everything in class, especially math." Terry finally looks up and she sees something in his eyes. "I don't," he says.

"And that is a reason to hurt her?"

Terry shoves his hands all the way down into his deep overall pockets and looks down again.

"And that is a reason to hurt her? Uncle Richard asks again.

"I guess not," mumbles Terry.

"You have two choices. You can come by my niece's house every Saturday for the next four weeks or we will go to the sheriff's office right now."

"No sheriff," mumbles Terry.

"Fine. I'll be there at one o'clock Saturdays, beginning tomorrow."

"Yes, sir," answers Terry.

Ree remembers how Uncle Richard had taught Terry math on her front porch every Saturday for the required four weeks. They had continued the lessons for weeks thereafter. Her Uncle Richard is no murderer.

## Chapter Five
*Sunday, October 21, 1962*

Ree has roped Aunt Maude into going with her to Oakland Cemetery down in Atlanta after church. Actually, Ree bribed her with the promise of onion rings and two chili dogs from The Varsity on the way home. It will be something to look forward to after the long drive.

"This is the craziest thing I've ever heard," says Aunt Maude. "Spreading your ashes to kingdom come and back."

"I couldn't agree more. But you know Aunt Clarisse. She danced to music we couldn't hear," says Ree.

"That's a nice way to describe her, Reeda."

Ree's thoughts turn back to the funeral and to Harold the moment he handed her Aunt Clarisse's will. He had been so rude. It infuriates her all over again.

"Aunt Maude, what do you know about Harold Perry?"

"I can tell you he is not related to the Lawrenceville Perrys. You may know one of them was mayor of Lawrenceville. Harold's people come from Florida. I understand he got his law degree from the University of Georgia and took the first job offer he received, which happened to be here in Lawrenceville. People here like him a lot. You know I hear people talk. They respect him. Say he deals fairly with them."

"Well, obviously they don't know how rude he is," says Ree.

"What was that? I didn't hear you."

"Nothing. Never mind." Changing the subject, Ree says, "I went to see the sheriff on Friday."

Startled, Aunt Maude says, "My heavens, why?"

"Every time I see Dad shuffling those postcards he gets every December, my heart breaks for him. So many unanswered questions. I thought it wouldn't hurt to do some checking."

"I don't think Richard had anything to do with your mother's death, Reeda. I don't want to shock you, but I think Richard loved your mother. He never came close to marrying anyone else, you know," says Aunt Maude.

"I've heard that before. I can't remember where I heard it. It certainly didn't come from Uncle Richard."

"Of course not. Richard was the picture of decorum. And he would never do anything to hurt James. I wish you luck with your quest. You know I will help if I can."

"You are helping today. Who else would spread Aunt Clarisse's ashes with me?"

\*\*\*

Ree helps Aunt Maude to the gravesite, which houses the remains of both Margaret Mitchell and the author's second husband, John Robert Marsh. Ree and Aunt Maude stand quietly, taking it all in.

"Aunt Maude, over to your left—that's where Loew's Grand Theatre stands. Lowe's was first constructed in 1893 as a grand opera house. In 1927 it was converted into an elegant movie theater. Of course, it's known for hosting the premiere of *Gone with the Wind*. What a night that was with Clark Gable, Vivian Leigh, and Olivia de Havilland all in attendance."

Taking a small nondescript jar out of her purse, Ree looks around to make sure no one is near Margaret Mitchell's grave. It felt surreal to be standing here with the ashes of her formidable aunt. *Should I say something? What do I say?*

"Ms. Mitchell, my aunt loved your book, *Gone with the Wind*, and, in her last words, she expressed her desire to have some of her ashes spread on your grave. She made it clear she thought Ashley a wimp and couldn't see what Scarlett ever saw in him, but she did love your book passionately. Frankly, I feel this is an invasion of your privacy, but here goes."

Ree gently shook the small jar back and forth to spill out ashes on the grave. Some of Aunt Clarisse's ashes settled over the grave while others spiraled up in the wind.

Ree and Aunt Maude stood reverently for a moment of silence until the city traffic sounds receded and were unnoticed by the two.

Aunt Maude broke their silence. "Reeda, would it be appropriate to say a prayer?"

"I think that is perfect. I'll pray. Lord, we thank you for the time we had with our Aunt Clarisse. She loved you, Lord, and, you know Lord, she danced to her own music. Please help us to honor her and remember her with love always."

Ree can barely hear Aunt Maude whisper, "Amen." She notices coins and stone in small piles on the headstone. Ree quietly reaches into her wallet and hands Aunt Maude a dime to leave on the stone.

\* \* \*

Coming home from Oakland Cemetery, they hear on the car radio that President Kennedy has decided on a naval blockade of Cuba. This shakes Ree's world. What will the blockage lead to?

## Chapter Six
*Monday, October 22, 1962*

Ree is in the kitchen, coffee in hand, enjoying the sun as it begins to peak over the top of her mother's café curtains. She is alone. It is so very rare that she is alone. Ree savors it, until she hears her father coming down the hall.

"Reeda, are you in the kitchen?"

Ree sighs, "Yes, sir."

James walks into the kitchen with a clear trash bag. A blood-soaked tee shirt that Ree recognizes as one she threw in the rag bin months ago is inside.

"What on earth?" says Ree.

"I think it's time you talk to your daughter, Reeda," says James.

"Why on earth?" says Ree, trying to find meaning to the bloody shirt.

Her father stands there, not responding. Waiting for the obvious to hit Ree. The Martin house only has one bathroom, and the three of them have few secrets.

Finally, he says, "It's Virginia."

It hits Ree. Hits her hard. Her daughter has gotten her first period, and she was totally unprepared for it. *What is wrong with me? How horrible can a mother be?*

Ree stands up and reaches for the bag. "I'll take care of it, Dad."

She walks upstairs to Virginia's room and finds her daughter still curled up in her canopy bed, a leftover from her great grandmother. Ree walks to the side of the bed and softly brushes the hair back from Virginia's forehead.

"We need to talk," says Ree.

Virginia untwists the sheets from her slim body and sits up. She notices the clear bag. She waits for her mother to say something.

"I am so sorry. I should have been prepared for this. I'm a horrible mother. Do you have questions? Do you understand what is happening to your body?"

Virginia looks up at her mother and grins, "Yes, I understand. I fell off the roof. And it's about time. All my friends have. I'm the last."

"But the rag pile?" asks Ree.

"It happened last night. You were asleep, I really didn't know what else to do."

"Well, at least I can take care of that before you go to school," says Ree. She starts to leave the room and turns back to really look at her daughter. There is more than one thing changing with this beautiful replica of her husband.

"Make sure you come straight home from school. I'll meet you here at four o'clock."

"You're leaving work early?" asks Virginia. "Why?"

"Because, my beloved daughter, we are going to Alford's to buy you some bras."

\* \* \*

Together they come down the stairs at Alford's—training bras in hand. Ree spots the senator's wife, Delia, coming into the store. She is preparing to greet her when Delia looks up suddenly and sees Ree and Virginia coming down the stairs. Delia quickly turns, and exits the store. She reminds Ree of a scurrying mouse.

*How very, very odd. I hardly know the lady… Surely she's not avoiding us.*

Ree's attention is diverted by Virginia. "Look, Mom, it's Sandy."

Sandy is a mechanical horse. He is saddle worn from all the children who have scrambled onto his back. Countless mothers have, through the years, put a quarter in the slot to watch their children gently rock back and forth on the smiling horse. Ree is no exception.

Ree freezes the image of Virginia and Sandy in her mind. Virginia is a toddler on Sandy's sandy-colored back in the freeze frame. But here she is in front of her at thirteen with one foot creeping into adulthood.

*Where has time gone? Why can't Mason be here to see their wondrous daughter?*

Ree wants to stand in the middle of Alford's and have a good cry. If she could, for just a moment. Just cry for the injustice of life and the fear she may never be enough for her daughter. The moment passes. Ree straightens her shoulders.

"Who wants a root beer float at Monfort's?" she asks.

"I do. I do," shouts Virginia.

Ree's heart settles. There is still some of that toddler left in her daughter.

\* \* \*

Settled in at the soda fountain at Monfort's, Ree and Virginia casually talk about school and other things Virginia is involved in.

"I haven't asked you," says Ree. "How do you like being at Central Gwinnett with all those upperclassmen?"

Virginia shrugs. "I like it. I like being away from the babies on the hill."

"But now you seventh graders are the babies, right?" says Ree, smiling.

"Maybe not such a baby anymore," says Virginia, holding up the bag of bras.

Ree laughs and bumps Virginia's shoulder. "Point taken," says Ree. "You and Margaret still enjoying junior majorettes?" Margaret has been Virginia's best friend all Virginia's life. Ree doesn't remember a time they weren't friends—always in and out of each other's homes.

"We love it, Mom. Did you know we may be able to go on the field at half time during the game against Cherokee this Friday? You and Granddad will get to watch us."

"Believe it or not, I do know that. It's on my calendar. And Granddad's, too."

Central Gwinnett Black Knights football reigns supreme during the fall in Lawrenceville. Ree and her family make it a point to go to all the home games. There's something to be said for the closeness of community when all the townsfolk are jammed shoulder to shoulder onto the icy cold metal stands, dressed in gold and black to honor the Black Knights.

Whether you intently watch the game, socialize with the people around you, or—if you are a child—constantly run up and down the bleachers, you are part of community. It feels special. After all, Ree learned in one of her college classes that after what Maslow described as the basic needs, such as food and shelter, are met, nothing is more important to humans than being part of a group. Central Gwinnett football games fill that need to a tee.

Ree spots the newspaper stand near the front of the store. The racks are filled with copies of *The Atlanta Journal*, *The Atlanta Constitution*, and *The Lawrenceville News-Herald*. She remembers she has stories due in the morning.

Virginia notices her mother look toward the stands. "Did you always want to be a journalist, Mom?"

"I honestly cannot remember when I didn't," says Ree. "What about you? What do you want to do with your life?"

"I want to write, too. But I think I want to write books, books about all types of people and events. I want to write about going to the moon one day. Or about Sacagawea. Or maybe even Martha Berry. Stuff like that." She smiles.

Ree fears the emotion bubbling up from her belly will choke her. *Her daughter, an author.* She wants to stop and explore the idea. Instead, she says, "And, tell me, why Martha Berry?"

"She made a difference. Truly. Her father was a wealthy man. But Martha was captivated by the poor children of sharecroppers and farmers. She made it her life's goal to educate as many of these children as possible. She taught them in a log cabin in her early years as a teacher and eventually opened a boarding school for boys and, later, one for girls."

Ree understands why her daughter would want to write about Martha Berry. A loud slurp tells her that Virginia has finished her float. It doesn't matter how many times Ree tells her not to, Virginia always slurps the end of her drink.

"Okay, kiddo. Time to go home."

\* \* \*

As she's walking down the hall toward the den, Ree recognizes the voice of President Kennedy coming from the radio.

"Ree, you and Virginia get in here right away," shouts James. "This is serious."

They walk into the living room to find Gus' and James' attention glued to the radio.

Gus looks up at Ree and Virginia. "Kennedy just said any nuclear missile launched from Cuba in the Western Hemisphere will result in the United States responding in an attack against the Soviet Union." Gus stops to draw a breath and continues. "The president is contacting the United Nations Security Council. He is asking for the withdrawal of offensive weapons from Cuba and the withdrawal is to be done under the supervision of the United Nations."

"Gus, be quiet. We need to hear this," says James.

Settling on the sofa, Ree pats the space beside her, motioning for Virginia to sit down. The four of them listen as President Kennedy continues:

> "...Seventh and finally: I call upon Chairman Khrushchev to halt and eliminate this clandestine, reckless, and provocative threat to world peace and to stable relations

> between our two nations. I call upon him further to abandon this course of world domination, and to join in an historic effort to end the perilous arms race and to transform the history of man. He has an opportunity now to move the world back from the abyss of destruction—by returning to his government's own words that it had no need to station missiles outside its own territory, and withdrawing these weapons from Cuba—by refraining from any action which will widen or deepen the present crisis—and then by participating in a search for peaceful and permanent solutions...

Gus interrupts and says, "We don't have any idea how horrible a nuclear war will be. If we do survive the blast, we will all probably get cancer." Gus sees the horror on Virginia's face and adds, "But I read we can shield ourselves inside a building of brick or concrete. That would reduce our exposure by fifty percent. That's...."

"Gus, damn it, be quiet. I would like to listen to President Kennedy, not you," says James.

A shocked Gus immediately stops talking.

> My fellow citizens: let no one doubt that this is a difficult and dangerous effort on which we have set out. No one can foresee precisely what course it will take or what costs or casualties will be incurred. Many

months in which both our patience and our will will be tested—months in which many threats and denunciations will keep us aware of our dangers. But the greatest danger of all would be to do nothing. ...

Our goal is not the victory of might, but the vindication of right—not peace at the expense of freedom, but both peace and freedom, here in this hemisphere, and we hope, around the world. God willing, that goal will be achieved.

**Thank you and good night."**

"So, we have begun a naval blockade of Cuba. Kennedy is asking for the withdrawal of weapons from Cuba. How will Khrushchev react? What do you think, Ree? I am afraid we have many frightening days ahead," says James.

Remembering Virginia snuggled beside her, Ree downplays her own fear. "President Kennedy is right: our worst option is to do nothing. What can the three of us do? Pray. Pray fiercely."

## Chapter Seven
*Wednesday, October 24, 1962*

Mr. Monroe and Ree are hashing things over in his office at the *News-Herald*. Ree understands that the country is holding its collective breath over the situation with Cuba. She wants to show how local people are impacted in her next article. This is a situation unraveling hundreds of miles away, but it is affecting people right here in Lawrenceville in any number of ways.

"But how do I do that, Mr. Monroe?"

"Well, for starters, you might want to talk to Nancy who works at the shoe store on Crogan. That's Keown's. She was scheduled to get married at First Baptist this Friday. The groom has finished basic training at Lackland Air Force Base in Texas, and the base, along with all the other bases in the country, are on alert. Nancy is marrying one of those Hudson boys—never can remember which one. Anyway, the groom has no idea when he will be home."

"Yes, yes, yes. That's what I mean. Thank you, Mr. Monroe."

"You can choose from any number of the Lawrenceville families who have sons in the military," says Mr. Monroe. "You know, Ree, we may never live through a scarier time. Soviet ships are nearing our blockade. I understand those ships are shadowed by a Soviet sub. It is the worst game of chicken you can imagine."

"I admit. I'm terrified," Ree says. She stands up, gathering her things. "If I'm going to meet tomorrow's deadline, I'd better get going."

\* \* \*

At Keown's, Ree finds Nancy shelving boxes of shoes. Ree remembers that Nancy lost her mother and her family home in a fire last year. Nancy and her father barely escaped and were now renting a home on Culver Street.

"Hello, Nancy. I'm Ree Jones, and I write for the *News-Herald*. I am interviewing people in Lawrenceville personally impacted by the Cuban Missile Crisis. I understand you had to postpone your wedding. Would you be willing to talk with me?"

"Would my words be in an article in the paper?" says Nancy.

"If you are willing, yes."

Nancy shelves another box of shoes and looks at Ree. "I guess it's okay. What do you want to know?"

"You had your wedding planned, is that right?"

"Yes, Sam and I—that's Sam Hudson—were to get married at the First Baptist Church on October 20. Sam is in basic training in San Antonio, Texas. All bases are on alert, and now I don't know when Sam can come home. I had mailed invitations, for gosh sakes."

"How horrible for you."

"Yes, I had to cancel everything. The church ladies were organizing a reception for us after the wedding. I had ordered flowers. The men took up a collection to send us to Gatlinburg for a short honeymoon, and I had made hotel reservations. All cancelled."

"I am so sorry your wedding day had to change and for all those changes you had to make …"

"That's not the worst by far. We could go to war. My Sam could go to war. I am praying on my knees every night—no war."

"I will get on my knees as well. I don't know if we have lived through a scarier time. Thank you for sharing your story with me, Nancy. I want our citizens to know how this crisis is affecting us locally. Your story certainly does that."

"You are welcome. I look forward to reading the other stories in the paper."

"And I look forward to receiving a wedding invitation from you. I would love that," smiles Ree.

## The December Postcards

\*\*\*

Ree makes a stop at the library on the way home. Dennis Forrester is there, shelving books in the fiction section. Dennis is what the townspeople call weird. Ree would never refer to him that way, but she can see why people do. Dennis has a bad habit of mumbling to himself. He certainly does look unusual with his pants pulled up under his arms, secured by a turquoise beaded Indian belt. His jet-black hair is highly creamed, parted in the middle.

Ree remembers Dennis and her mother were once friends. She approaches him tentatively. "Hello, Dennis. I am picking up a book for my dad. Can you help me?"

Dennis puts down the book he's holding and, moving to the circulation desk, says, "Yes, ma'am. We have Mr. James' request all ready."

Digging in a bin behind the desk, Dennis finds *Advise and Consent* by Allen Drury and brings it to the counter. "How is Mr. James?

Ree smiles at Dennis, touched that he has asked about her father. "He's just fine, Dennis. Thank you for asking. You know, I'll tell him you asked about him."

"That would be fine. Just fine," says Dennis.

"Well, thank you, Dennis."

"Yes, ma'am. And you have a good evening."

\*\*\*

## The December Postcards

Ree is on the way out of the library, thinking Dennis was rather loquacious tonight, when she barely hears him whisper, "I remember your mother." Ree feels chills along her spine. How creepy.

Dad's postcards are still spread out on the coffee table. Dinner can wait. Ree sits down on the sofa to peruse the collection of cards postmarked Paris, London, Edinburg. She spots postcards from points across the United States—Amelia Island, San Antonio, Washington D.C.

She groups the cards by location, sorting them into piles for Europe, the western part of the United States, and the deep South—not far from their Lawrenceville home. Postcards from the southern states have arrived postmarked from North Carolina, Alabama, Florida, and Georgia. From Alabama, they have come from the cities of Point Clear and Tuscaloosa and from the small town of Marion. From Georgia, she sees postmarks from Jekyll Island and St. Simons. From Florida, there are cards from Miami and Amelia Island. And the last postcard from the southern United States is postmarked Asheville, North Carolina.

Ree assumes the postcards are from Richard. If she can use the postcards in some way to find Richard, then maybe she can solve the murder. Ree doesn't think Richard is the murderer, but he may know who is. Maybe that's why he's still on the run.

*Is he protecting someone? What does he know?*

# The December Postcards

She picks up the postcard from Amelia Island. No personal clues here. Just a visual of blue skies, white sand, and a reddish sun hanging low in the sky above the clear waters.

Ree remembers Louise, her friend on Amelia Island. Louise is a prolific writer of mystery novels and has long had a home there. Ree visits once a year, usually in November. So, it's nearly time. *Why not visit now?* She could leave on Sunday afternoon and come back on Tuesday. Ree reaches for the heavy, black phone to set things in motion just as the doorbell rings.

Going to the door, she peeks through the sidelights and sees Miss Gladys Witherspoon standing on the welcome doormat in front of the door, casserole or something in hand. In Ree's opinion, Miss Gladys is after James big time. And why not? James is lonely, and Miss Gladys is attractive with her shift dresses and high heels. Not a varicose vein on those legs.

Ree opens the door. "Why, hello Miss Gladys. So nice to see you."

Miss Gladys peers around the door, looking around. "Oh, I just brought one of my meat loafs. You know, I add veal and ground beef. My mother made it that way, and she is the best cook in…."

Interrupting, Ree says, "Why, thank you so much, Miss Gladys. Dad is not here, but I know he'll appreciate your meat loaf. He really gets tired of my tuna casserole."

"You say James is not here?"

"No, he's out with Gus somewhere."

"Well, I'll just get back home then," says Miss Gladys. "Nice to see you, Reeda."

"Nice to see you as well, Miss Gladys."

Ree watches Miss Gladys, ankles wobbling, turn and go down the steps and then onto the sidewalk. Why does she wear those high heels anyway? Ree thinks it's to show off those legs. Oh, well. If you got it, flaunt it.

\*\*\*

Ree is in the kitchen when she hears James come in the front door. "I'm in the kitchen, Dad," she yells.

As James enters the kitchen, Ree says, "Guess what's for dinner? Meat loaf made by your honey."

James frowns. "My honey?"

"Don't be coy with me, Dad. I'm talking about Miss Gladys."

"I don't know about her being my honey. She takes a meat loaf to Gus, too."

Ree laughs. "She's hedging her bets, huh?"

"Don't know about that. I do know the lady can cook."

"Oh, come on Dad. You know she likes you. And what's not to like?"

James grins.

## Chapter Eight
*Thursday, October 25, 1962*

The *News-Herald* comes out today, and Ree and Mr. Monroe are checking the proofs for errors.

"Ree, I like your story about the monument on the courthouse square—the one dedicated to the 1836 Battle of Shepherd's Plantation with the Creek Indians," says Mr. Monroe.

"I wanted to write the story for this issue because of the dead bodies. Somehow, dead bodies on the courthouse lawn fit in with Halloween. There are eight Gwinnett men buried under that monument. They fought in the bloodiest battle fought with the Creek Indians," says Ree.

"Did you know one of those eight men was a Martin? Could be a relative of yours."

"I noticed that, but I'm afraid it's research for another day."

"Now, we have the stories about the Halloween parade and the carnival, right?"

"Yes, I covered both of those. The parade is tomorrow afternoon at 1:30. All the witches and monsters and goblins from

Lawrenceville Elementary will parade through the streets of Lawrenceville."

"And the carnival?"

"It's Saturday night at the elementary school gym from 5:30 until 9:00."

"Don't you ever think about leaving the *News-Herald* for one of those big Atlanta papers, Reeda. I simply could not survive without you. Now, did you see the story by Bruce Still and Mrs. Betty Cole, the women's coordinator for Civil Defense? It ties in with the local interviews you conducted about the Cuban Missile Crisis."

Ree turns the paper to the front page. The headline, "The Role of Civil Defense More Important Than Ever; Families Asked to Plan," leaps out at the reader. The article indicates that most citizens are coming to the realization of the potential not just of war but of a nuclear war.

"This terrifies me, Mr. Monroe. Look. Citizens are advised to have seven gallons of water per person available in their homes. Stay inside our homes and have a two-week supply of non-perishable food on hand."

"Not since Pearl Harbor have people been so afraid. It is a good thing that we have the parade and the carnival to keep us busy. We do have to go on with our lives, but there has never been a time to be more prepared."

"Speaking of going on with our lives, I need to take Monday and Tuesday off. Is this possible?"

"Of course. All you do is work. I hope you are going somewhere for fun."

"Oh, I am. I am going to Amelia Island to visit my friend, Louise."

"You're not going to miss the carnival, are you?"

"I wouldn't do that to Virginia. The carnival is one of those things in her life you don't mess with. She loves everything about it. I'm not leaving until Sunday after church. It's a flying trip."

"Well, God speed, Reeda. And have a wonderful trip."

## Chapter Nine
*Saturday, October 27, 1962*

The carnival is in full swing when James, Virginia, and Ree walk up the hill to the elementary school. There's a bite in the air. Leaves swirl in the slight breeze. Children's laughter rings through the crisp evening. Music from fiddles, raucous and friendly, provides the perfect backdrop for the annual festivities.

Virginia can hardly contain herself. She rushes ahead to the steps leading to the gym basement. Ree is startled to hear Virginia scream, then she remembers you have to run the gauntlet of goblins and monsters going down to the spook house. High school boys delight in terrifying anyone walking down the stairs.

Ree and James avoid the spook house as they have no desire to feel squishy intestines and slimy eyeballs or to face monsters lurking in the dark recesses of the school. They head straight for the gym.

It's not long before Virginia, along with her friend Margaret, come up to the gym to explore bobbing for apples, getting their fortunes told, and "fishing" which involves throwing a line from a fishing pole over a curtain that looks suspiciously like a bed sheet in the hopes you will hook a glorious prize. Excitement bubbles up as you feel a tug on the line. Before you know it, you are pulling back a pole with a small doll or metal car on the end.

James' friend, Gus, comes up to their group. Gus had been the principal at Central Gwinnett High School years ago. He has long since retired, making way for the current principal, William Martin, who fits somewhere in James' lineage. James is not quite sure where. Gus just has to compare the current state of affairs at the high school to the days when he was principal. Of course, everything was better when he was in charge.

"You know, when I was principal over at the high school, I worked with the elementary school to have a much better carnival. Oh, well," says Gus. "Things change, don't they?"

"Oh, get off it, Gus. Let's go check out the cake walk," says James.

"Okay, Okay. Nice to see you, Reeda," says Gus.

"Nice to see you, Gus. When are you coming for dinner? You promised me you would," says Ree.

"Soon. I promise, soon," says Gus.

The two men walk off, speculating on what cake Miss Gladys has baked, and Ree is left alone. What an odd time to remember her Uncle Richard, but she does, thinking back to the carnival the year she turned eleven, Ree remembers how none of her classmates voted for her for Miss Halloween Princess. She knows this because she heard Miss Grace Thomas tell Miss Alice Carver that Ree was the only girl in the entire class who did not get at least one vote. And why would she? A tall girl with big ears that stand straight out from her face. And big feet to match.

Ree remembers taping her ears to her head once, thinking they would lie flat, if she could just keep them taped. Ree remembers how gently her mother removed the scrunched, dirty tape from her head.

Sensing her mood, Uncle Richard had told her she was the most beautiful girl there. With her thick, red hair and her straight nose showered with freckles she knew it couldn't be true. But when Uncle Richard said it, she believed it. He reminded her that while she was showing respect for others, she must do the same for herself.

"Show some self-esteem, young lady." She had never forgotten those words. Or how he loved her.

Ree has nothing but warm, wonderful memories of Uncle Richard. She remembers playing games with him on the front porch. He always sprinkled in little life lessons during their time together. Lessons like walking in a girl's ballet shoes before judging her. Even better, don't judge people, period. Another was never, ever lie.

Would Uncle Richard be tsk-tsking because she told Miss Grace she liked her dress? An obvious lie.

Harold Perry, of all people to see today, interrupts her thoughts of Uncle Richard. Ree has not seen him since her attempt to apologize failed before she could utter a word. Harold accused her of having an "elevated opinion of herself." His exact words, Ree believes.

"Uh, Ree, I think it's my turn to apologize, if you'll let me."

"You were pretty nasty to me, Harold."

"I know. I know. There's just something about you, Ree. I lose my filter. Anyway, I am apologizing now. I was horrid. I admit it. Will you accept my apology?"

"Why, thank you Harold Perry. I think I will. But you have to square dance with me first."

Harold frowns. Not what he was expecting.

Ree laughs. "Come on, Harold. Let's give it a try."

\* \* \*

James promises to keep an eye on Virginia, so Ree accepts Harold's offer to walk her home. She hasn't even packed for her trip to Amelia tomorrow. That's all that's on her mind.

"Penny for your thoughts," says Harold as they walk down Perry Street toward the square.

Ree puts thoughts of Amelia Island away and smiles at Harold but says nothing. She admires the courthouse with its multi-storied clock tower and remembers the stately ballroom on the second floor with its vintage chandeliers and tall ceilings. She looks around at the shops on the square, like McConnell's Five and Dime store and Wilson's, the best place to shop for wedding gifts. She thinks about all the people that work in the shops, and she smiles because of their friendliness and open hearts.

"I am thinking about how I love this town," says Ree finally.

"I love it, too. Just look at these misshaped pumpkins lining the street. They will be replaced soon with colorful turkeys and pilgrims taped to the storefront windows," says Harold. "At first, I thought people were just friendly to me because of my last name. I later found out that wasn't true. They would have been friendly to me regardless of my name."

"You mean they thought you were related to Mr. Jim Perry, mayor here in early 1900s?"

"I didn't know about him. I meant Perry Street. There had to be some significant Perrys at some time in Lawrenceville's history."

Turning to walk down Pike Street, Ree sees the Methodist church in the distance. Her family had been members there for decades.

"Harold, do you think our faith will guide us if we go to war?"

"Why, yes, I do. I know it is scary. One of our U-2 pilots was shot down over Cuba today. That alone is bound to accelerate the move toward all-out war. I don't know what's coming but, I tell you, I pray about it."

"It's that dang Castro. He's all but begging Khrushchev to launch a nuclear strike against our country. Thank goodness Khrushchev has ignored his pleas, so far. But this business about the U-2 pilot moves us to another stage," says Ree.

Harold stops walking and looks at Ree.

"What?" she asks.

"I am finally lucky enough to spend time alone with you, and all we have talked about is war."

Ree laughs, stands on her tiptoes, and kisses Harold on the cheek. "We'll do better next time."

Harold smiles. Next time. She said there would be a next time.

"Good night, Harold. I promise, no more yelling at you."

"Good night, Ree. Until next time."

\* \* \*

As Ree is getting ready for bed, she thinks of Mason. What would he think about her walk with Harold? Ree thinks he would be rip roaring furious with her for kissing Harold.

*How does she feel about it?* She will always love Mason. *Always.* But she sorta likes the idea of seeing Harold. *What does that make her? Unfaithful? Surely not.*

Ree thinks she'll move this question to the back burner for now. She has to pack. She leaves for Amelia Island in the morning.

## Chapter Ten
*Sunday, October 28, 1962*

Sunday morning finds Ree, James, and Virginia in their familiar pew at the Methodist Church. As the congregation stands to sing the Doxology, Ree reaches for Virginia's hand. She squeezes her daughter's small hand as they sing together:

> **Praise God, from whom all blessings flow;**
> **Praise him all creatures here below;**

Ree settles in her place on the pew, along with the rest of the congregation, as Reverend Foster steps up to the pulpit. "Good morning, congregation. I am fortunate to be the pastor here at Lawrenceville Methodist," says Reverend Foster. "If you are new to our church, please meet me here at the altar after the service. I want to welcome you and get to know you. Now, I have been forced to change my sermon this morning, but confess I am thrilled to do so."

Parishioners look at each other with raised eyebrows and frown lines on their foreheads. *What in the world?*

"I have life-altering news," says Reverend Foster.

Ree along with the rest of the congregation sucks in her breath.

"Khrushchev has announced he will dismantle Soviet missiles in Cuba," says Reverend Foster.

You can actually hear the whoosh sound as the congregation releases its collectively-held breath. Ree immediately realizes what this means. No threat of nuclear war hanging over their heads. No need for bomb shelters and gallons of water and non-perishable food. This means Nancy, who is marrying one of those Hudson boys, will have her wedding.

"CBS broke the story right before the service started. President Kennedy agreed to pull our missiles out of Turkey, if Khrushchev will do the same in Cuba," says Reverend Foster "And, since we are doing everything out of order on this splendid morning, let's stand and sing the 'Gloria Patri.'"

> **Glory be to the Father and to the Son**
> **and to the Holy Ghost;**
> **as it was in the beginning,**
> **is now, and ever shall be,**
> **world without end. Amen. Amen.**

"I cannot think of a more perfect way to praise God for this miracle," says Reverend Foster.

\* \* \*

After church, Ree is in her bedroom putting the last few things she'll need for the trip to Amelia in her suitcase. She's got to get on the road to the Atlanta airport. As it is, she'll be meeting Louise in Jacksonville after dark.

Virginia peers around the door of Ree's bedroom, then walks in and sits on the bed.

"You'll be back Tuesday?" Virginia asks.

"Yes, dear, and I have something to tell you, if you can keep a secret," says Ree.

"Cross my heart," says Virginia.

Ree smiles, remembering she said the same thing when she was Ree's age.

"You know I am going to see Louise on Amelia Island?"

"Yes," says Virginia. "You go every November."

"This time I am going for a special reason. One of the postcards your granddaddy received is from Amelia. Odds are I'll find nothing, but it's worth a try. Two birds with one stone. I'll have a great visit with Louise as well."

Virginia stands up and hugs Ree around the waist.

"I'll miss you, Mom."

"I'll miss you, too, sweetheart."

## Chapter Eleven
*Monday, October 29, 1962*

Over coffee and bagels Monday morning, Ree and Louise plan their day on Amelia Island. They agree on a morning at the beach, catching up and working on their tans. The air has cooled, but this is Florida and temperatures have been warmer than usual.

"Let's shower and get dressed around noon and go downtown. We can eat fried shrimp and walk it off going into the shops of Fernandina Beach. What do you think, Ree?"

"I love it. I'm going to put this pasty body into my swimsuit right now."

Louise laughs. "You are a little pasty, girl. We'll work on that."

\*\*\*

Settled in their beach chairs, Ree says, "You are one lucky lady. If I ever leave Lawrenceville, this is where I'll be."

"Would you consider leaving if you were alone?"

"No, my soul is at home in Georgia. Besides I may have met a man." Ree says this, knowing the shock value her statement has and waiting for her words to land with her friend. It doesn't take long.

"A man?" says Louise.

"Yes, a man. His name is Harold. He is a local lawyer, and I like him. He stuck around after I yelled at him on the streets of downtown Lawrenceville. But he's no pushover. He told me my opinion of myself is highly overrated. He said I think every man under fifty wants to jump my bones."

"My goodness, I think I like him, too. Do you think men want to jump your bones?"

"I assure you, it's the furthest thing from my mind."

"So, where do things stand with this Harold?" asks Louise.

"It's a work in progress. We're just beginning, really."

"And what about Virginia and James?"

Ree smiles. "Virginia is the spitting image of Mason, and she's strong. She keeps me on track."

"And your father?"

"Not so well. I've told you before about the mysterious postcards he receives every December. Last December, he didn't receive a card, and he constantly worries about the missing card. He hasn't said as much, but I know he thinks the cards are from Richard. He thinks something has happened to his brother."

"The whole thing is so terribly sad and mysterious," says Louise.

"That it is. Let me add to the mystery. One of the cards was mailed from here, from Amelia Island," says Ree.

"Seriously?"

"Yes. I have decided to try to solve the Richard mystery, but how in heaven's name will I find out about his stay at Amelia?"

"I see what you're saying: a needle in a haystack. Enough for now. I'm starving, so let's go find some fried shrimp."

\* \* \*

Stuffed full of shrimp, fries, and slaw, Ree and Louise saunter down the streets of beautiful Fernandina and soak in the history. They city has flown under eight flags since the 1500s and, even with its bright and clean modern-day hotels, restaurants, and shops, you just know so many years of historical Fernandina is to be found there in the shadows.

Louise tugs on Ree's sleeve. "Come on. This is the best store on the island, and not only because they carry my books."

Louise is referring to The Book Corner, a quaint book store that looks just how a perfect book store should look, with nooks and crannies and shelves filled with all sorts of books.

"Good," says Ree. "I must admit I failed to buy your last mystery. This is a good time to correct that."

Searching through the mystery section of The Book Corner, Ree finds Louise's latest book and takes it to the register to purchase. After fumbling in her purse for money, Ree looks up at the tall, brunette lady behind the register. She catches a glimpse of a framed picture behind the bookstore clerk. To her utter astonishment, she sees it is a photograph of her Uncle Richard.

Ree grips both hands on the wooden counter in front of her. She squeezes even harder, trying to keep her balance. *Am I going to faint? I never faint. My gosh. It is Uncle Richard.*

Louise hears the brunette ask Ree if she is okay. She hurries around the corner to find a pale Ree gripping the counter for all she's worth and staring wide-eyed at a picture on the wall. Louise notices a name under the picture: Richard Todd.

"Ree, come with me. I don't know what is wrong, but you need to sit down," says Louise.

The brunette, wearing a name tag that identifies her as Mary, says, "Please, please, sit down. I'll get you some water." Mary leads Ree to one of the chintz-covered armchairs in the store's bay window.

Recovering, Ree thanks Mary as the bookstore clerk hands her a paper cup filled with water. After taking a sip, Ree straightens up and asks, "Mary, what do you know about Richard Todd, whose picture is on the wall behind your counter?"

"Oh, Richard. He's an island favorite. He lived on Amelia for almost a year, researching American Beach. We have a copy of the excellent non-fiction book he wrote about the area."

"Are you still in touch with him?"

"We used to get a postcard every year. Funny, we didn't get one last year."

"Please add Mr. Todd's book to my purchase. Mary, I apologize if I scared you. I think the island shrimp didn't agree with me."

Ree gathers her belongings, pays for her books, and thanks Mary one more time. As they exit the store, Louise drags Ree to one of the wooden benches that line the sidewalk.

"Now talk," says Louise. "You can eat a truckload of shrimp. What was that all about? It certainly wasn't a reaction to shrimp."

Ree looks down, contemplating how best to tell Louise. She looks up at Louise. "That picture of Richard Todd? Todd is my Uncle Richard's middle name. That picture is of my Uncle Richard… And what is American Beach?"

I can do better than explain American Beach to you. I can *show* you American Beach," says Louise. She and Ree drive out of town headed toward the south end of the island. "American Beach was founded by Abraham Lincoln Lewis in 1935, so blacks could have a place to go to the beach."

"Well then, I can see Uncle Richard being interested. He hated segregation—no blacks on beaches, public pools, restaurants. You know, I hate it, too," says Ree. "But who is Abraham Lincoln Lewis?"

"He was Florida's first black millionaire and the president of an insurance company."

"Well, good for him—building this American Beach."

"You know, I came to Amelia as a child. My family came every year and our maid, Mattie, came with us. She stayed at American Beach."

Louise turns left onto a sandy road that leads to the beach. Small houses colored blue, turquoise, and cream are lined up in rows. The lucky owners live in the ones that face the beach. Ree rolls down the window to breathe in the wonderful salty smell of the beach.

They drive by Cowart's, a motel and restaurant with the unmistakable scent of fried fish wafting in the air. There are several night clubs, Rendezvous and Ocean-Vu-Inn, that offer dancing and dining.

Ree is lost in thought. Her heart aches that such a place as a beach for blacks has to exist. "I think I've seen enough, Louise," she says. On the short drive back to Louise's home, Ree tries to imagine her Uncle Richard at American Beach. He would be saddened, too, that a place like American Beach had to exist in this country.

## Chapter Twelve
*Wednesday, October 31, 1962*

Ree catches her father before he heads over to Edge's to have breakfast with Gus.

"Dad, come have a cup of coffee with me. I need to talk to you about my trip," says Ree.

"Sure," says James. "Did you have a good trip? And how was Louise?"

"Yes, and good," Ree smiles at her father. "Dad, you know one of the December postcards was from Amelia Island?"

"Oh, yes. I've memorized the location of every card. Why? What about it?"

Ree reaches down beside her chair where she has propped the book on American Beach. She hands the book to her father.

"American Beach?"

"Look at the back cover, Dad."

As James takes in the picture of Richard, Ree watches as the muscles in his jaws tighten. He seems to freeze. His head is down. His eyes are transfixed by the picture of Richard.

## The December Postcards

"Dad?" says Ree. She's worried. Should she have handled this differently?

"How in heaven's name, Reeda? How did you find this? Was this book published after Richard left Lawrenceville?"

"It was published in 1950 and, believe it or not, is still in print. In its second printing, I think. What's the date on the postcard from Amelia Island?"

James leaves the room and comes back with the postcards fanned out in his right hand. He sits down at the kitchen table and pulls the Amelia Island card out of the pack. Turning the card over, James says, "1950."

Ree grabs her father's right hand with both of hers and squeezes. "We found him, Dad. And look what he is accomplishing. This book contains rave reviews about his work."

"I have always believed the postcards were from Richard, but there is no explanation for last year—no card."

"Well, we are going to track him down. Then we'll know."

"We?" says James.

"Yes. All of us. You, me, Virginia. I'm looking at Tuscaloosa now, and I will probably take Virginia with me. After that, we'll all go wherever the cards take us."

"I'll tell you, Sug, you give me hope. That's something we all need desperately. I love you, Reeda. I need to tell you more often. Something else, you do a wonderful job taking care of Virginia and me. You need to hear that, too."

Ree stands up and walks to James. She kisses him on the forehead and walks out of the kitchen. Ree lets the tears run without bothering to wipe them away.

*   *   *

After breakfast and with her fresh face on, Ree enters the *News-Herald* building. Of course, she can't make to her desk without hearing comments from Miss Betty and Miss Mary. Ree thinks of herself as a modern warrior running the gauntlet with her desk as the goal.

"Did my eyes deceive me or did I see you leave the carnival with that handsome Harold Perry?" says Miss Mary.

"Well, that's fantastic. You've finally wised up, huh Ree?" Miss Betty chimes in.

Ree blows the two busybodies a kiss and sails through the room, swerving left to head toward the storage room.

Once at the sagging wooden desk, Ree again opens the book with copies of issues from the year of her mother's death. She swishes through several editions of the *News-Herald*, scouring them for some mention of Billy Faucett. She chooses more books from the shelves.

In one of them, she finds an article in an April edition of the 1936 paper about a murder in Snellville. An elderly lady found dead in the sanctuary of the Baptist Church. Cause of death: a blow to the head with a blunt instrument.

## The December Postcards

In the January edition of the following year, 1937, a shop owner in Lilburn was found dead in her store. Cause of death: a blunt force instrument. The murder had remained unsolved.

Ree works on piecing together all she's learned about Billy Faucett and the other murders in the years around her mother's murder. She overlays that information with what she knows about her mother's death. Faucett escaped the year her mother was murdered. The timing fits.

Skipping lunch, Ree works on her latest article assignments for the *News-Herald* until it's time to go home and get ready for Halloween. There's nothing like Halloween on the square. She wouldn't miss it for the world.

\* \* \*

Halloween is the most wonderful of holidays, Ree thinks as she got dressed for the evening. First of all, the weather is perfect. Cool enough for layers of warmth under your costume. Next, spookiness abounds. Trees with bare arms reaching skyward add to the ambience. Leaves crunch underfoot. *Do I hear someone following me?* Yes, it is a spooky, creepy holiday, and while it's mostly for children, it's still glorious. And nowhere was it more glorious than right here in her hometown.

Virginia has been excited for weeks: she and Margaret have been talking costumes for weeks. Margaret is going to be a colonial girl. Her costume, top to bottom, was ordered from the

Sears and Roebuck catalog and features a dress with a skirt of yellow taffeta and a parasol. Virginia is going as Cinderella, dressed in one of Ree's first prom dresses and a tiara from her wedding to Mason. Her little girl is wearing makeup for the first time tonight. Ree adds blush to her cheeks and bright red lipstick to her lips.

James, with Gus' help, will be giving out candy at home while Ree takes Virginia and Margaret over to Forest Hills subdivision. Walking out to her car, Ree is thrilled to see a group that includes Batman, Superman, Casper the Friendly Ghost, and an astronaut headed toward her home, where James and Gus are rocking on the front porch.

*Next year*, Ree swears to herself silently, *we'll decorate the house with pumpkins, scarecrows, fake spiderwebs—the works.*

Ree starts the car. The sounds of "Monster Mash" flood the car. WLAW is playing Halloween tunes tonight, and the girls sing along in their loudest, finest voices.

As she turns into the Forest Hills subdivision, Ree pulls up along the curb on Maple Wood Drive to let the girls out. She will follow them in the car as they walk from house to house with their pillowcases—soon to be filled with candy bars, suckers, jaw breakers and, if they are lucky, nickels and dimes.

After the girls trick or treat at several houses, two boys catch up to them. The four of them continue to trick or treat together. Both boys are dressed as hobos. The girls obviously know them. They are laughing and having a good time.

Ree watches them like a hawk. Who is this beautiful Cinderella looking up at a handsome hobo?

"Good grief," says Ree aloud. It may be time to worry about boys. *It's just too much. It's just too fast.*

## Chapter Thirteen
*Friday, November 2, 1962*

Ree is working on articles for the November 8 edition of the *News-Herald* when Mr. Monroe walks up to her desk.

"Hey, Reeda, are you working on the Dottie Hurley story?" asks Mr. Monroe.

"Yes, and I have to say I am loving writing this story," says Ree. "Imagine, our first female candidate for public office, running for mayor no less."

"And it seems she is running with the full approval of Mr. Hurley," says Mr. Monroe.

"Yes. I love that, too. Did you hear the story of how she entered the race?" asks Ree.

"Something about a hat?" says Mr. Monroe

"Oh, yes. She announced her candidacy by placing her beautiful, feathered hat on the desk at city hall."

"Don't tell me she said, 'My hat is in the ring.'"

"Yes, she did. She certainly did," says Ree.

"Well, it makes for a great story for the *News-Herald*. You know Rhodes Jordan is running as well?" says Mr. Monroe.

"That is my next story," says Ree. "Balanced reporting, always."

"I could use five more just like you, Reeda. Don't let that Harold Perry take you away from us."

Ree groans. "Not you, too, Mr. Monroe."

Thinking of Harold Perry, Ree remembers. He is picking her up at six o'clock for their first date.

\*\*\*

Harold has chosen his favorite Chinese restaurant for their first night out together. It's in downtown Norcross across from the train depot. *Norcross is perfect*, Ree thinks as she looks at the menu. This far from home, there's little to no chance of gossiping hens from Lawrenceville who might spot her and Harold dining out.

Over sizzling rice soup, Harold gives Ree a full rundown of his love of Chinese food. "Every Sunday, without fail, my aunt and I went out for Chinese after the church service. That lady tried every dish on the menu many times over, and she loved every one of them," he says.

"Tell me about her—your aunt," says Ree.

"She was a saint, if you can picture a saint that is short, round, with an apron tied around her middle. I've never known a person who could spread so much love."

"She was very important to you?"

"Yes, but it's a sad story. Let's don't tell it tonight."

Ree picks up her glass and clinks it with Harold's. "I agree. No sad stories tonight. You loved going to the University of Georgia?" she asks.

"Gosh, yes. That's why I'm a double dog." He smiles, waiting for her to ask.

"A double dog?"

"Yes, two degrees from UGA."

Ree laughs. "Well, you have me beat. Just one degree in journalism for me. I tell you, I love that campus. The day I finished my last class, I walked slowly around North campus. It was a walk of love for UGA.

"I wish I had known you at Georgia. I think we would have had a fabulous time there." As they finish up their main dishes, Harold asks Ree about spreading Aunt Clarisse's ashes.

"Aunt Maude went with me to Oakland Cemetery. We spread her ashes on Margaret Mitchell's grave, just as she requested."

Harold leans back in his chair and laughs out loud. "I would give anything to have seen that."

"It wasn't funny. I expected someone to arrest us at any minute."

After Harold finishes another round of laughter and gains his composure, he asks, "So, what is next?"

"Spreading ashes under the rose bushes at church."

Taking pity on Ree, Harold says, "How about I help you?"

"Great. We can both go to jail."

Harold grins, visualizing the two behind bars as the waitress approaches, bringing the bill and fortune cookies.

"I love fortune cookies." Ree cracks open the crisp cookie and pulls out the fortune tucked inside. She reads: *You will soon cross the wide waters.*

"What does it say?"

"I'll cross wide waters. I hope that means I'll finally get to Europe. What does yours say?"

Harold blushes. *My gosh, he's turning red. What on earth does it say?*

"So, what does it say?"

"Be ready when love walks in the door."

Ree smiles at him.

Harold puts down cash to cover the bill, and they walk outside. Not a person in sight. Harold turns Ree to him and kisses her. Ree has forgotten how very spectacular it is to be kissed. She kisses him back.

## Chapter Fourteen

*Sunday, November 4, 1962*

Virginia and Margaret are at the church for a Methodist Youth Fellowship meeting, as are most Methodist youth on Sunday nights. It is a great time for young people to get together to socialize under the umbrella of faith. The meetings always end with the singing of "Blest Be the Tie That Bind." They all stand to sing:

> **Blest be the tie that binds**
>
> **our hearts in Christian love;**
>
> **the fellowship of kindred minds**
>
> **is like to that above.**

As the song ends, Bill Anderson, a freshman at Central and the hobo with Virginia on Halloween night, whispers to the teenagers standing around him, "Hey, I hear you can climb up in the clock tower at the courthouse. Would that be cool, or what? I think we should do it."

"Nah, we're going home," says one of the Bower twins. "We could get in serious trouble."

"I'm in," says Sam Weaver.

"Virginia and Margaret?" asks Bill.

Virginia answers for both of them. "Sure. We'll go," she says.

Margaret's eyes go round at the thought of climbing the tower, but, like her friend, she doesn't want to be chicken—afraid to climb a measly little tower "Yes, we'll go," echoes Margaret.

"Cool," says Bill. He leads the way out of the church and toward the town center.

* * *

To get to the clock tower the foursome have to enter the courthouse at the Crogan Street entrance. Once inside, they take the stairs on the left to reach the second floor.

"And why do we want to do this?" asks Sam, as they arrive on the landing.

"Shush," says Bill. "Lower your voice. The police check on the courthouse. Do you want them to hear us?"

Virginia and Margaret look at each other with frowns at the mention of the police.

Bill motions the group toward the small wooden door that leads to the clock tower. They hold their collective breaths as he turns the doorknob. The door is unlocked. Bill flips the light switch on the wall just inside the door. Facing them is a high, narrow set of dusty wooden stairs that lead upward. Spiders have spun their webs in the corners of the steep steps, adding to the spooky atmosphere.

"Here we go," says Bill.

Graffiti covers the dingy white walls on either side of the staircase. Virginia is reading the names and slogans on the wall to her right as she climbs the creaky stairs. She is followed by Margaret and Sam. Virginia suddenly stops, causing Margaret and Sam to bump into her. She is taking in what is carved on the wall, eye level with her.

*Tommy loves Ree.* There is a heart carved around the words. Virginia tears up. Her mother and some boy once did exactly what she is doing now, maybe at the very same age. How odd, and wonderful, to think of her mother at her age.

"Go on up, Virginia," says Sam. "What's with you?"

Virginia quickly wipes away a tear and moves up the steps and into a small room with old brick on the walls and narrow recessed windows overlooking the now dark downtown streets. To the right is a long ladder leading to the clock itself. Virginia shudders, but follows Bill up the ladder.

Once at the top, Bill says, "My friend's grandfather takes care of the clock. See these weights? When they hit the bottom, this crank has to be turned to take the weights back up to the top. It takes eight days for the weights to travel from top to bottom. Then they have to be cranked to the top again."

"Hey, you, up there! This is Sheriff Pitts. Come down from there right this minute."

Virginia freezes. *The sheriff. Oh, no. Will he take us to jail? My mother is gonna kill me.*

"It's me, Bill Anderson. We're coming down, sheriff."

Bill leads the others down the steep stairs to meet the sheriff. Sheriff Pitts' mouth flies open at the sight of Virginia and Margaret. He slowly closes his mouth only to open it again and says, "What the heck are you young girls doing out at night with these boys? And up in the clock tower to boot?"

Before Virginia can answer, Bill speaks up. "It's my fault, sheriff. I wanted to see the clock tower. I talked them into it. All my fault."

"Well, that's gentlemanly of you, Bill, but it doesn't take the blame off the others. As for you two girls, I'm taking you home to your parents. Boys, I'll deal with you later."

Virginia and Margaret still have not spoken one word as Sheriff Pitts walks them across Clayton Street to Virginia's home. The sheriff knocks on the door several times before Ree opens it.

"What in heaven's name?" says Ree.

"I found Virginia and Margaret up in the clock tower at the courthouse with two boys. Sorry to bring you the bad news, Reeda," he says.

Ree looks at Virginia and Margaret. She's never seen two more penitent souls.

"Thank you for bringing them home, sheriff. Will there be any charges against them?"

"Knowing you and James, Reeda, I'm sure any punishment you dish out will suit the law just fine. I'm taking Margaret home. I'll leave Virginia to you."

As Sheriff Pitts walks off, Margaret in tow, Virginia meekly follows Ree into the kitchen.

Without blinking an eye, Ree says, "What were you thinking?"

Virginia opens her mouth to speak, then closes it.

"Virginia?"

"We just wanted to see the clock tower, Mom."

"Did it enter your head to ask permission?"

"No ma'am."

"And the two of you being out at night with two older boys? What do you think that looks like, Virginia?"

Virginia doesn't know how to answer. This is a side to her mother she rarely sees. Mad as all get out and totally in charge.

"Go up to bed, Virginia. I assure you there will be consequences for your actions. The first consequence will be no more MYF on Sunday nights. That group is too old for you and Margaret."

"Mom, please. No."

Reeda stares her daughter in the eye until Virginia turns, crying, and runs upstairs to her bedroom.

Ree sits at the kitchen table. She bends her head down until it almost touches the table. *See, God. I'm not good at this parenting thing. In fact, I'm horrible. Please help me.* Ree starts to cry—big, gulping cries.

Virginia hears her mother's cries. She slides her flannel gown over her head to muffle the sound, but when it doesn't work she gets up and goes down to the kitchen doorway.

"Hey, Mom," says Virginia. "I love you." Virginia turns quickly and runs back to bed.

## Chapter Fifteen

*Monday, November 5, 1962*

Ree and Virginia are eating warm oatmeal in a chilly environment. It is obvious to Virginia that her mother is still furious with her. Ree has yet to say good morning or give Virginia her usual morning kiss. She just slams the bowl of oatmeal on the table and sits to eat.

After long minutes have passed, Virginia puts her spoon on the table and looks at Ree. "Mom, I know you are mad at me. I admit it was a stupid thing to do, but I knew I'd be safe with Bill. You just don't know him, Mom."

"Well, I tell you, I don't think highly of a boy who will take a thirteen-year-old girl up in the clock tower. You all had to know the clock tower is off-limits."

Virginia looks her mom in the eye. She is still for a moment. Finally, she says, "Mom, did you ever go up in the clock tower?"

It's Ree's turn to be uncomfortable. She squirms in her chair. Fidgets with her long hair. Ree looks at Virginia and says, "Yes."

Just the one word, *yes*.

"I just want to tell you, Mom—going up the steps to the clock tower—I saw a heart carved into the wall. Inside the heart was written, 'Tommy loves Ree,'" says Virginia.

All the anger and frustration Ree was experiencing went poof. Ree gets a dreamy look on her face. She tells Virginia the story as she gazes off into the distance.

"I was your age. Tommy was my first boyfriend. Tommy knew how to get to the tower. Coming down the steps after seeing the clock, he stops in front of me, turns, and kisses me. He takes out his pocket knife and carves 'Tommy loves Ree' on the wall inside a heart."

"Mom, that is so romantic. Did you kiss him back?" says Virginia.

"Wouldn't you just like to know?" says Ree. "Come here." Ree opens her arms wide.

Not caring that she's too old, Virginia sits on Ree's lap and hugs her tightly. All is right. Lifting her head from Ree's shoulder after a few minutes, Virginia asks, "Do I really have to drop out of MYF?"

"Yes, that group is too old for you and Margaret."

During the night, when she couldn't sleep, Ree had decided. She would plan a Sunday night meeting for the thirteen and fourteen-year-olds. She is not telling Virginia yet. She doesn't want Virginia to get off the hook so easily. Ree turns Virginia's head toward her and kisses her on the forehead.

## Chapter Sixteen
*Saturday, November 10, 1962*

It's a Saturday and the town square is packed with people. Old men sit on the low wall surrounding the courthouse, chatting about the day as children skate by on the sidewalk that surrounds the courthouse. Women with grocery lists head into Alford's for Saturday shopping.

Mother and daughter cut across Crogan Street. A few smiling pumpkins from Halloween remain. Drawings of pilgrims and fall leaves have been added to the store window display. It's early November and Christmas is already beginning to swirl in the minds of the people of Lawrenceville, but no whiff of Christmas decorations until after Thanksgiving. It's an unspoken rule.

Just as Ree and Virginia pass Saul's, Ree hears a voice from behind them. "Mrs. Jones, may I have a word with you?" She turns to see a man with Bill, the boy from Halloween and the instigator of the clock tower shenanigans, in tow. The two walk briskly toward them. Ree steps over to the outside wall of Saul's to get out of the mass of people on Crogan. Following her, Mr.

Anderson says, "Mrs. Jones, I am Jim Anderson. Bill's father. I believe Bill has a few words to say to you."

"Mrs. Jones, I owe you and Virginia an apology. I am so sorry I got Virginia in trouble. It was all my idea, going up in the clock tower. I guess I just didn't think."

Ree is impressed with Bill Anderson. He looks her straight in the eye while delivering the apology. He seems sincere. Like he knows what he did was wrong.

"I hope you won't punish Virginia," he adds. Bill looks at her daughter, who gives the appearance of being totally mortified by this scene, a red blush on her cheeks. Her eyes are downcast, firmly fixed on the street.

"Well, Virginia is being punished. She knows right from wrong. Thank you for the apology, Bill." Turning to Mr. Anderson, Ree says, "Thank you, Jim. I hope it is okay—my calling you Jim. I have a feeling we will run into each other again." Ree smiles at this last comment. "Oh, and please call me Ree."

"Thank you, Ree," says Jim. "Hopefully, no apologies will be involved the next time we meet."

"I agree with that," says Ree. "I hope the rest of the day is better for you two. Come on, Virginia. Let's get to Monfort's."

Virginia looks back at Bill as she and her mother walk away. Bill smiles at her. *Okay. Maybe everything will be okay.* Virginia smiles back.

## The December Postcards

\*\*\*

The Georgia-Florida football game blasts throughout Monfort's as Ree and Virginia enter the store. It is the most important game of the season, and many Lawrenceville residents travel to Jacksonville for the game.

Virginia and Ree say hello to the two high school boys working as soda jerks at the grill situated on the right of the store. You can get a great grilled cheese here. The smell of melted butter hangs in the air as you walk through the door.

Virginia stops to look at the comic books while Ree heads back to the pharmacy. She picks up her prescription, then moves to the front of the store where she hears, "The Dawgs are going to mess around and lose this game. I'm mad. That's how I am. That Johnny Griffith couldn't coach my grandmother."

"Georgia losing?" says Ree.

"Yes," grumbled one of the men.

"Well, you know the Dawgs will pull it off. Goodbye, gentlemen." Leaving Monfort's, Ree and Virginia bump into Dennis, who works at the library.

"Hello, Dennis," says Ree.

"Hello, Miss Reeda. Is your father enjoying *Advise and Consent?*

"I'm sure he is. Good to see you, Dennis."

"I miss your mother," says Dennis.

Surprised, and suddenly recalling his statement the day she picked up the book for her father, Ree hesitates before saying, "I miss her, too."

"I take flowers to her grave. Not all the time. But some of the time," says Dennis.

Standing in place, Ree flinches slightly. Finally, she says, "I know Mother loves your flowers, Dennis. Thank you for doing that."

Dennis stares off into space, then repeats, "I miss your mother."

*How strange.* Ree leaves him staring at her blankly and quickly collects Virginia. The uneasy feeling she has after her encounter with Dennis follows her down Perry Street and past Wilson's where elderly men play checkers on a table set up on the sidewalk. The uneasy feeling follows her all the way home.

## Chapter Seventeen
*Sunday, November 11, 1962*

Ree, James, and Virginia are seated in their usual pew at the Methodist Church. *How is it Sunday already?* Ree thinks. Their pew is halfway down the middle section on the right. This Sunday has special meaning to James: it's Veteran's Day.

James won't talk about the World War II years, but Ree knows from Aunt Maude that her father had joined the Royal Air Force to help England fight against Nazi Germany. Volunteers from the United States formed squadrons during the time the United States remained neutral in the war. James flew as a member of an Eagle Squadron until 1942, after our country entered the war, when he transferred into the United States Army Air Forces.

Sitting in the sanctuary, Ree looks at her father. She tries to imagine him flying in fighter and bomber escort missions.

Her thoughts are interrupted when the senator and Delia walk down the aisle and seat themselves a few pews in front of Ree and her family. Senator Scott, the perpetual politician, smiles and shakes hands as he comes down the aisle. He is followed by Delia, who hardly smiles at anyone.

Ree knows a little about the Senator's background, mostly from his own political fliers. He went to the University of Georgia where he met Delia, whom he married just before winning his first election to the Georgia Senate in 1934. He had entered the Navy just as the United States joined the Allied effort to stop Germany's aggression in 1941.

Once seated, the senator turns to smile at James and his family. James nods. Ree smiles back. They settle in to listen to the sermon.

The Methodist Church shares the tradition of honoring veterans by having them stand as their branch of the service is called. It's a special day of the year for Ree—watching her father stand when they announce the Army branch. So many men in the congregation stand. Ree sees these U.S. Army veterans as proud, distinguished warriors. Without fail, she tears up. This year is no different.

The senator stands when the Navy is announced. There is a fair representation of Navy men in the congregation today. The senator continues to stand after the other Navy men sit down. Ree hears a few snickers. Delia grabs his coat hem and gives it a tug. He sits down reluctantly.

After the service, the senator stops to speak to James. "James, every time I drive by the Feely house, I think of you and

## The December Postcards

Mildred. What a horrible thing to happen. I was out of town that day, but I remember how the town grieved. Mildred was a wonderful lady."

James nods at the senator, steps out of the pew, and walks down the church aisle and out the church doors. Ree is left to handle the awkward situation. What was the senator thinking, his condolences so out of place?

Ree says, "Thank you for your concern."

The senator frowns and grabs Delia's elbow. "Good day, Reeda. You, too, Virginia," he says. The senator struts down the aisle, his wife on his arm, nodding and smiling as he makes his way.

Ree just stands there. Something the senator said is off, but she can't think what to save her life.

## Chapter Eighteen
*Monday, November 12, 1962*

Ree wakes up thinking about the church service yesterday and the odd encounter with Senator Scott. The senator won his State Senate election in 1934 and went on to serve two more two-year terms as a Georgia senator. It was rumored he wanted to run for governor in the years following his service in the Georgia Senate. Evidently, he couldn't get the backing he needed.

*What was it the senator said that bothered Ree so much?*

Maybe it would come to her. She had a full day of interviews and planned to spread Aunt Clarisse's ashes in the rose garden on the side of the church tonight. Better get up and get going.

Brushing her hair before going down to breakfast, it comes to Ree. The senator said he was out of town on the day her mother was murdered. But Sheriff Pitts had told her there was a statement in her mother's file from Senator Scott. He had stated that he had seen Richard's car in front of the Feely House on the day of the murder.

*Strange. Strange, indeed.*

\* \* \*

James answers the door to Harold's knock.

"Come in, Harold. Come on in the living room. Gus and I are playing a game of chess. Do you play?"

"I play a game similar to chess. Afraid I'm not very good," answers Harold.

"Well, we need to have a game some night. We'll see how well you play."

Gus chimes in, "Good to see you, Harold. You know, when I was principal at Central Gwinnett, we had a chess team. We were the first high school in the state to have a chess team. I'm very proud of that."

Trying not to smile as James rolls his eyes, Harold says, "I'll bet you are, Gus."

At that moment, Ree walks into the room.

"Come on, Harold. I'm rescuing you from these two."

"Where are you off to?" asks James.

Ree places her index finger over her lips before saying, "It's a secret. I can't tell you."

"Is that Clarisse's urn you got under your arm? Whatcha gonna do with that?"

"You do not need to know. I promise you." Ree pulls Harold by the arm out of the room and out the front door. They walk around the corner to the rose bushes.

Harold stops and, taking the urn from Ree, puts it on the ground. "Come here," says Harold.

Ree walks into his arms, and he kisses her. Pushing back, she says, "Harold Perry, you can't kiss me on the street in plain sight."

"Aw, Ree. Your reputation is safe. I checked. No one is around. I wouldn't be spreading ashes with you if anyone was around."

"Good point. Okay, let's do this."

Just as when she was at Oakland with Aunt Maude, Ree felt the need to say something about her Aunt Clarisse. Or for her. That verse, 1 Corinthians 13 seems appropriate tonight, she thinks.

Ree paraphrases, "Love is patient, love is kind. It does not envy, it does not boast, it is not proud." She stops. She is thinking about her mother, instead of Aunt Clarisse. Her mother was all about love. She spread it freely. Ree can't go on.

Sensing this, Harold picks up where Ree stopped. "When I was a child, I talked like a child, I thought like a child, I reasoned like a child. When I became a man, I put the ways of childhood behind me." Skipping a verse, he finishes, "And now these three remain: faith, hope, and love. But the greatest of these is love."

# The December Postcards

Listening to Harold recite the verses, something moves deep inside Ree and breaks into a thousand bright lights. She is beginning to care about this man. No doubt about it.

Ree kneels in front of the rose bushes and tips the urn on its side to release Aunt Clarisse's ashes. She spreads the ashes around the base of the roses, remembering how her Aunt Maude told her they were Confederate Roses—called that because bouquets of them were given to Confederate soldiers returning from the war. Ree is surprised at how pleasant this task is. She rubs her hands in the soil, seeing the gorgeous blooms above her in red, pink, and white, their smell so sweet.

Ree finishes and stands up, just as a car pulls up. *My gosh. It's Miss Betty Holland.* Ree takes her right foot and kicks the jar containing Aunt Clarisse under the rose bushes.

Miss Betty reaches over and rolls down the window on the passenger side of the car. "Well, what are you two up to? Taking a romantic stroll?"

Ree would like to strangle her. How embarrassing.

Harold says, "Just taking a walk around town. Would you like to join us, Miss Betty?"

Ree kicks him in the shin.

"Thank you, Harold, but I have to get home to the husband. You two take care." They hear her laughing as she rolls the passenger window up.

"I will never be able to work with her now," says Ree.

"For gosh sakes, Ree. Don't let her get to you. Tell her I was jumping your bones."

Ree hits him on the arm. Then she laughs out loud. The whole scene is just too funny.

"Let's walk around the square, and I'll tell you the story of my life," Harold says.

Ree takes his arm. They start down Pike Street. "I'm all ears. But I have a question."

"Shoot," says Harold.

"How did you know the verse from 1 Corinthians? I have to say I am impressed."

"My Aunt Merry raised me and the old saying about going in the church every time the doors open applied to Aunt Merry. That meant it applied to me as well. Before you ask, I can guess your next question. Why did I live with my aunt? Long story short—my father left my mother for another woman when I was five. My mother committed suicide, and Aunt Merry took me in."

The similarity in their stories hit Ree. Hard. "Harold, I lost my mother, too. She was murdered."

Harold squeezed her hand but said nothing. They walked almost an entire block before speaking.

Ree broke the silence. "It was hard, wasn't it?"

"Yes. I had to listen to well-intending church-goers tell me my mother couldn't go to heaven because she committed suicide. No child needs to hear that."

"That's horrible. How did you overcome it?"

"My Aunt Merry and, funny enough, our pastor. My Aunt Merry cornered every lady that told me that and gave them what for. Our pastor did the same, in a more subtle way. The comments stopped, but I still remember that five-year-old child and how he felt."

"Again, that's horrible."

"Yes, but after that, the church took me in. I was smothered with love. I am still friends with a lot of the kids who were in my Sunday school class back then. They come to Lawrenceville from time to time."

"And the law?"

"Although I am a general practice attorney, I am especially interested in divorce law. I've always wanted to help women like my mother. I love to do that."

"I think you are an admirable man, Harold Perry."

"Ditto to you, the honorable Ree Jones. Now, I think I better walk you home before I really do ruin your reputation right here on the Lawrenceville Square."

\* \* \*

Snuggled into bed, Ree is reliving the night in her mind. It will be worth Miss Betty's teasing to have more nights like this with Harold. Miss Betty…

*Oh, good grief. Aunt Clarisse is still under the rose bushes. I better retrieve her. Good grief.*

## Chapter Nineteen
*Wednesday, November 21, 1962*

Edge's on Clayton Street is known for its T-bone steaks. Both James and Gus are indulging heartily, each of their steaks cooked to perfection. They both requested medium rare.

"Gus, I've known you a long time, and I've never known you to spread gossip. So, can you keep a secret?"

"I'm insulted you asked. Of course, I can."

James puts a bite of steak in his mouth and chews before answering, "I've been getting postcards every December since Mildred died. I think they are from Richard. I didn't get one last December, and it has me really worried."

"James. Who knows about this?"

"Just Ree and Virginia. And Maude."

"But postcards? Where are they from? What do they say?"

"There's nothing written on the cards, and they are postmarked from all over the United States and Europe as well."

"They're blank?"

"Yes, blank. Now Ree has decided to track some of them down, and I'm going to help her."

"My gosh, James. This has been going on all these years, and you never told me?"

"Can't you see I couldn't? If the postcards are from Richard, I need to protect him. He did not murder Mildred. That's one thing I know for certain. I think Ree thinks if she finds Richard, she may find out who murdered Mildred."

"I'm honored you told me, James. I'll tell no one. You can be sure of…."

"Well, good afternoon, gentleman. Good to see you. How are those steaks?"

James and Gus look up to see the senator standing at the end of their table.

"The steaks are the best. You know that. How are you, senator?" says Gus.

"Never been better. Good to see you two." The senator nods and walks off.

James eats his last bite of steak and wipes his mouth. "Now, are we going to eat some butterscotch pie?"

"Not me," say Gus. "I got to get over to the high school. I think they want me to help the football coaches during practice."

*I'll just bet they do.* James says nothing about what he is really thinking.

Picking up the check and standing up, Gus says, "I've got it this time, James." As the two leave the restaurant, Gus turns to James. "That Dennis Forrester is one strange human being."

"What brought that up?" says James

"He was in the booth right behind us. Didn't you see him when we walked out? You need glasses or something?"

"I have glasses, thank you. And, as for Dennis, Mildred liked him. I never could understand why. I think he's a little odd myself. Anyway, thanks for lunch, Gus. I'll get you next time."

"Sure enough." Gus walks toward his car.

"Hey Gus, why don't you come for Thanksgiving dinner tomorrow?" yells James.

Gus yells back, "I am. Reeda invited me weeks ago."

\* \* \*

Walking up Clayton Street, James sees Reeda and Miss Gladys talking on the front porch. Miss Gladys spots James and squirms all over, like a wriggling puppy. When James reaches the ladies, Ree says, "Dad, look. Here's Miss Gladys to see you, and she brought us a sweet potato casserole for Thanksgiving."

"Oh, James. I am so glad I didn't miss you. You know I always make my sweet potato casserole for Thanksgiving, and I thought, 'Why don't I make James one, too?' I know you will just love it. I bake my own sweet potatoes and mash them with orange juice. No canned yams for me. Never. My mother would turn in her grave if I used canned sweet potatoes. And…."

Before Miss Gladys can catch another breath, Ree says, "Wonderful to see you, Miss Gladys. I hope your Thanksgiving is wonderful. Now, I've got to run."

"Really?" says James, a look of desperation on his face.

"I'm going by the cemetery, Dad. Then I'll run by the *News-Herald*. I'll be home before too long. Have to get my casseroles going. Thanks to Miss Gladys, I won't have to make a sweet potato one."

Ree smiles at Miss Gladys, hugs James, and makes a beeline for her car. She continues to smile at her father's discomfort. *How did he ever catch her vivacious mother?*

\* \* \*

Ree drives into the cemetery off East Pike Street and turns left in the direction of Mason's grave. She kneels at the headstone engraved with Mason's name and his birth and death date. To the right on the tombstone is a space for her information when she goes to join Mason. It's eerie to Ree, and she chooses not to dwell on it.

Ree remembers the first Thanksgiving she and Mason shared —her first turkey, which turned out fine, and her gravy, which did not turn out fine. After she scraped her gravy into their new gravy boat, a wedding gift from Aunt Maude, it refused to come out. Mason even turned the gravy boat upside down. It still wouldn't come out. Ree tried to not be offended when her husband had roared with laughter. She remembers Mason pulling her onto her lap after dinner and telling her what a wonderful dinner it was. Ree smiles at the memory. She misses him.

Ree tells Mason about spreading Clarisse's ashes under the rose bushes. Leaving nothing out, she tells him about Harold walking with her around the square.

"Mason, you are my love," she says softly. "The father of my wonderful daughter who is growing up faster than you would like. I have to tell you, I am beginning to have feelings for Harold. The funny thing is, Mason, I think you and Harold would be great friends. I think you'd really like him."

Ree sits back on her haunches and listens for a comment from Mason. She waits. She hears only the wind as it whistles through the large oaks and, in the distance, traffic on Highway 29, busier by the day.

Remembering the stones at Margaret Mitchell's grave, Ree searches and finds a smooth stone near Mason's grave. She kisses it and places it on top of Mason's headstone, before she turns and walks away.

## Chapter Twenty
*Thursday, November 22, 1962*

Thanksgiving Day. It was finally here: Ree's favorite day of the year. Hugs when guests walk in the front door. The front door decorated with a wreath of yellow, red, and gold leaves. Everyone talking all at once over a turkey and dressing meal, the anticipation of Christmas swirling in the air around them.

Harold is the first to arrive. He follows Ree into the kitchen where he takes her in his arms and kisses her.

"I am thankful for you, Reeda Jones."

"I am thankful…"

Gus interrupts by walking in the kitchen unannounced. His hair is slicked back, and he is sporting what looks like a brand-new cardigan over a blue dress shirt. Very cosmopolitan. After hugging him, Ree steps back to look him over, then says, "Aren't you looking spiffy, Gus. What's that you're carrying?" The dish looks vaguely familiar to Ree.

"It a sweet potato casserole. Miss Gladys made it for me, and I thought I'd share it."

"Wonderful, Gus." Ree just can't resist. "Just put it on the sideboard in the dining room by the sweet potato casserole Miss Gladys made for Dad."

Gus frowns, obviously confused. Then he looks at Ree and just grins.

Gus is followed by Mr. Monroe from the paper and his wife, Peggy. It has been a tradition for years that Ree's boss and his wife join them for Thanksgiving dinner.

Aunt Maude is the last to arrive with deviled eggs sprinkled with paprika. Virginia walks up just as Aunt Maude arrives. Hugging her, Virginia says, "I'll take those for you, Aunt Maude. Is there anything else? Do you need help?"

"I have a cranberry salad in the car. We need to get it in the refrigerator until we eat. Oh, and I brought a sweet potato soufflé."

Ree smiles. It's her turn to hug Aunt Maude. "It all sounds wonderful. Daddy will get those out of the car. Come in. Come in."

\* \* \*

The group gathers around the dining room table that Ree has decorated with cranberry-filled martini glasses. Each is topped with a small, lit tea candle. The glasses are scattered down the center of the long cherry table. Magnolia leaves and plaid ribbon are interwoven around and between the glasses.

James sits at the head of the table. Before saying grace, he looks at the empty chair on his right. It's Mildred chair. They always leave it open at family gatherings. It's a way to remember the vibrant mother and wife they miss so much.

James always says the same blessing, whether it's Ree, Virginia, and him having breakfast or a big family gathering, such as Thanksgiving.

> **Lord, bless this food to the nourishment of our bodies and our lives to your service. Amen.**

There is no lack of chatter around the table as plates are passed to James for a serving of turkey. Then the other dishes are passed around the table, with extra helpings of sweet potatoes available to all. Ree sits still for just a moment, taking in the wonderful people gathered around the table and the savory smells of Thanksgiving. The scents of turkey and gravy, turnip greens, and sweet potatoes mix with the sights and smells of cranberry sauce, fresh yeast rolls, and cheesy squash. Thanksgiving has a unique smell, she thinks.

Ree loves the chatter, too. Mr. Monroe and Peggy talk over each other, recounting in great detail the tale of their first Thanksgiving in Lawrenceville. Harold and Gus exchange comments about UGA football. James explains to Virginia how to carve a turkey.

It is a wonderful mish mash of chatter, good food, and love. Ree is jerked back to reality when she realizes she and Virginia leave for Tuscaloosa in the morning.

## Chapter Twenty-One
*Friday, November 23, 1962*

The postcard from Tuscaloosa, dated 1953, lies on the hotel bed between Ree and Virginia. The postcard features sites on the University of Alabama campus, including Denny Chimes, a bell tower built in the 1920s on the Alabama campus to honor the University's president George Denny. Ree picks up the card and turns it over. Of course, no personal message. Still, just holding the card helps her feel a connection to her Uncle Richard.

And the prayer is that she will do just that—*make a connection*. Now that she and Virginia are here in Tuscaloosa, it certainly seems possible. Ree made the reservation for herself and Virginia at The Stafford Hotel, the finest accommodation she could find in Tuscaloosa, weeks ago. Now they were here.

The Stafford, originally built in the early 1800s as a female academy, is a landmark in Tuscaloosa. It is a nine-story hotel with air-conditioning. Its slogan is, "Where you can expect the best." Ree picks up a matchbook from the bedside table in their hotel room and discovered from the writing on it that the hotel has a snack bar, dining room, and a beautiful new lounge. It is the dining room Ree is interested in. She and Virginia have lunch scheduled for tomorrow with a professor from the University.

Last week, Ree had contacted the University of Alabama Social Studies Department. After explaining to the receptionist that she wanted information on someone who taught in the history department in the 1950s, she had been referred to the head of the history department, Dr. Bryan Martin. He has agreed to have lunch with Ree and Virginia on Saturday at the Stafford Hotel.

Until then, she and Virginia are going to hit the streets of Tuscaloosa to see what they can see. First up will be Denny Stadium, where Bear Bryant coaches one of the best football teams in the land.

\* \* \*

Ree and Virginia are seated in the dining room of the Stafford Hotel, looking at the menu options.

"I am going out on a limb here. I am assuming you are Reeda and Virginia from Lawrenceville."

Ree looks up to take in the tall man standing before them —hat in hand, wearing a bolo tie and cowboy boots. Surely this is not Dr. Bryan Martin, professor of history at the University of Alabama?

"I am Bryan Martin. We have a lunch date?"

Flustered and stifling her instinct to comment on his appearance, Ree says, "Yes, Dr. Martin, thank you so much for agreeing to meet with us. This is my daughter, Virginia. And, please, call me Ree. Everyone does."

Seating himself, Dr. Martin says, "I wouldn't have missed this lunch. Richard is my friend."

Ree feels the tension in her shoulders releasing. "Wonderful. Did you teach together here at the University?"

"Yes, we did. May we order first, before we talk? I have a two o'clock class. Even though it's Saturday, I'm working with a group of students. I can't be late. It sets a bad example." He smiles.

Ree and Virginia had already decided on **Turkey à la King**, to be followed by dessert. Dr. Martin orders and thanks the waitress, then turns to Ree.

"Richard and I taught together here in the history department. I landed in the department from Wyoming beginning in 1946. I got a lot of ribbing. Dr. Martin looks down at his boots and smiles. When he joined the department, Richard always defended me. We became great friends, and—I tell you—no one could make history come alive like Richard."

"I am so glad you were friends. We have worried so about him. It is very hard on my father, Richard's brother."

Virginia asks, "You are a Martin. Are we related?"

"The two of us laughed a lot about the possibility, but we never did the research to prove it, one way or the other."

"I am so glad you were friends. Do you know anything about his past?"

"Some. I think he was accused of something he didn't do. It ate at him, and he missed his family terribly."

"He never told you anything more specific about why he left?"

"No. He came close one time, but never did. He told me the sheriff from his hometown hated him, so he could never go home."

Ree and Virginia looked at each other. This is news.

"Did he explain?"

"He told me he testified against the sheriff's brother in a murder trial, and the sheriff never forgave him. Even though the brother was guilty and was sentenced to life in prison."

Ree puts her fork down, and frowns. This may explain why Richard felt he had to leave Lawrenceville. The sheriff would probably assure Richard did not receive a fair trial. How horrible for Richard.

"Do you hear from him after he left the University?" asks Ree.

"I did, but he never revealed more about his past. Or his present either. We talked about our days at the University."

The waitress walks up to the table to take their dessert orders.

"I highly recommend the pecan pie," says Dr. Martin.

"Virginia, would you like pecan pie?" asks Ree.

"Of course," says Virginia.

"Make that three," says Dr. Martin.

"Can you give me some idea about Richard's situation? Is that asking too much?" says Dr. Martin.

Ree hesitates.

"Tell him, Mother. Everyone in Lawrenceville knows," says Virginia.

"You are right, Virginia." Turning to Dr. Martin, Ree says, "There is no reason not to tell you. Richard was accused of murdering my mother in 1934. His cane was the murder weapon, and it was found by Mother's body. He was jailed, but before he could be tried, he escaped."

Dr. Martin was riveted. "And you have not heard from him in all those years?"

"Not a word as to whether he is alive or not. My father has received a postcard every December since Uncle Richard disappeared. The postcards are posted from various locations, here and abroad. They are totally blank. Dad has always felt they were from Richard. We had no idea until recently that he had taught here at the University of Alabama."

"I imagine you think Richard is innocent?" says Dr. Martin.

"I know he is. The Uncle Richard I knew would never take a life."

"I agree on that point. I couldn't agree more." Dr. Martin glances at his watch. "I am so sorry, but I have to get to class. Are you staying for the night?"

"No, we are leaving to head back home after lunch. I can't thank you enough for taking the time to meet with us, Dr. Martin. I think you have explained a huge piece of the puzzle."

"Glad to do so." Dr. Martin rises to leave. "Virginia, when you are ready for college, come to Alabama. I'll give you a tour. It has been a pleasure for me to meet Richard's family. I can see why he missed his family so much."

Ree and Virginia sit at the table long after Dr. Martin leaves, trying to absorb what they just learned. All those years, Uncle Richard was right here in Tuscaloosa, teaching history.

## Chapter Twenty-Two
*Monday, November 26, 1962*

Pouring a morning cup of coffee for James, Ree says, "I need to talk to you about Richard."

James turns a kitchen chair around, straddles it, and rests his arms on the top of the chair back. It flits in Ree's mind that James is putting a barrier between him and Ree.

"I want to tell you what I learned in Tuscaloosa," she begins. "Dr. Martin told me the only time Richard came close to opening up to him was when he mentioned that the sheriff in his hometown hated him. He said he couldn't go home. Tylor Croft's name came up. He was sheriff when Mother was murdered?"

"Yes, the son of a bitch. He was."

"What's the story there, Dad?"

"Sheriff Croft's brother was a scoundrel. Buddy was his name. Buddy and his cousin, Dan were playing cards with Sam Moore in an upstairs room at the hotel. Buddy accused Sam of cheating and, long story short, shot him. Richard saw Buddy and Dan coming down the stairs that night and testified at their trials. Both Buddy and Dan went to prison. Sheriff Croft sure had it in for Richard."

"So, Richard would not have gotten a fair trial in Lawrenceville?" asks Ree.

"That's my opinion," says James.

Ree gets up and kisses James on the forehead. "That is so sad. And it makes me angry."

"I know, daughter, I know."

"I'm off to work, but I am coming home a little early. I am decorating this house for Christmas tonight."

James smiles. "I would love to help, but I'm sure Gus and I have something to do."

Ree smiles back, "How convenient."

\*\*\*

James and Gus find the perfect Christmas tree. They position it in the front window of the living room. They even add the traditional red, green, and blue light bulbs. Ree stands in the middle of the living room and takes it all in—the cedar tree with its clustered needles and the string of colored bulbs waiting to be plugged in. They will add a multi-colored glow to the room and bring it to life.

Ree remembers Christmases past and senses the assurance hanging in the air that Christmas will come again, bringing with it wonder and love.

# The December Postcards

"Mom," Virginia yells down the stairs. "I'm bringing down the decorations from the attic. Come help."

Ree feels warmth in her heart. She had planned to put on some Christmas music and do all the lifting, carrying, and decorating by herself. *Family. They always come through for her.* "I'm coming," Ree yells back as she takes off her coat and puts down her purse.

In the attic she uncovers box after box of tree decorations, as well as pictures, candles, angels and other items used to decorate the entire house. When Ree and Virginia finish stacking the boxes from the attic and carrying them down the steps, they start decorating the tree—first with ornaments Mildred helped Ree make when Ree was a child. Ree's favorite features a red Santa hat atop a man with a beard and a smiling face drawn on the egg-shaped ornament. Ree and Virginia add colorful glass birds with stiff nylon string for tails, ornaments that represent the states and countries James and Mildred visited early in their marriage, and round glass bulbs with colorful stripes around their middles.

Ree plugs in the lights and Virginia claps with excitement.

Next, they take the five-candle window decorations with their towering middle candles and two candles on each side in descending order. The candle sets go on the sills of all windows facing the street.

Lastly, Ree looks at the pictures to be hung in the living and dining rooms. There are six embroidery-designed framed pictures that represent different Christmas scenes. These were embroidered by Mildred's mother. *Priceless.*

Ree walks to the wall where the pictures hang every year and places her fingers in the nail holes that mark the location of each picture. She remembers her mother hanging these very pictures when she was a child.

*Tradition… Such a beautiful way to keep her family's traditions alive.*

## Chapter Twenty-Three
*Saturday, December 1, 1962*

Saturday morning finds Ree and Virginia in the kitchen making Aunt Beth's chocolate chip cookies. Aunt Beth Martin is a relative Ree has never met, but she feels like she knows her because of James. Every year at Christmas time, James mentions Aunt Beth and her wonderful recipes. The chocolate chip cookies include coconut, chocolate chips, oatmeal, and pecans. They're the best.

As Ree sifts the flour and baking soda, she remembers her mother taking cookies to Dennis. In the spur of the moment and in the spirit of Christmas, she decides to do the same.

"Virginia, we are going to take cookies to Dennis at the library."

"Why on earth would we do that? He's weird, Mom."

"We are doing it because Mother did. And because it's Christmas."

\* \* \*

Ree and Virginia walk across Clayton Street and enter the library.

"Hi Dennis. I've brought you some of Aunt Beth's cookies. The ones Mother always brought you."

Dennis brushes the hair off his face before taking the plate of cookies from Ree. He doesn't say anything for a moment, making Ree uncomfortable. He's looking at the cookies, as though he's pulling up memories of Mildred bringing them to him.

"Mom, is it okay if I run on to Monfort's to get a cherry soda?"

"Yes, I'll join you in a minute," says Ree.

"You know they argued," says Dennis.

Turning from Virginia back toward Dennis, Ree says, "I'm sorry, Dennis. What was that?"

"Your Uncle Richard and your mother had a big argument. They were on the sidewalk in front of the courthouse. They were so loud. Everyone could hear them. I remember. I was scared."

It's Ree's turn to say nothing for a moment.

"What did they argue about?" says Ree.

"I don't know. I just remember they both looked really mad."

"Oh," says Ree.

"Lots of people heard them. Miss Gladys. Miss Catherine Evans. The senator's wife, Miss Delia."

"Thank you for telling me," says Ree.

Remembering his manners, Dennis thanks Ree for the cookies.

Ree wishes Dennis a Merry Christmas and moves on to Monfort's fountain where she finds Virginia talking with some teenage boys, one of them being Bill Anderson.

"Hello, Mrs. Jones." Bill smiles.

Ree smiles back. "Nice to see you, Bill. Virginia, if you have your soda, we had better get moving. I need to buy a hostess gift for Aunt Maude. Her open house is tomorrow."

Virginia blushes. She has forgotten to order her cherry soda.

Ree smiles again. "You know, I think I'll have one of those cherry sodas you mentioned, Virginia. Make that two, Bill."

Turning to Virginia, Ree says, "And we really do have to hurry. I've got to get to Wilson's."

Walking to Wilson's for a hostess gift, Ree and Virginia pass clusters of people gathered on the sidewalk. Most of them are talking about the mayoral race. Lawyer Rhodes Jordan has defeated runner-up Dottie Hurley to become Lawrenceville's new mayor. Ree thinks Rhodes Jordan will make a great mayor but thinks Dottie Hurley is a winner in her own way.

*A woman running for mayor. About time.*

Ree loves walking into Wilson's this time of the year, mainly because of the Christmas china. There are shelves near the front of the store filled with it: the traditional china with the

Christmas tree in the middle of the plates and children's toys heaped at the base of the tree. Ree loves it. She tries to buy one new piece every December.

But today it's all about Aunt Maude. What can she buy for her aunt? Ree spots an oval glass bowl and thinks of the pretty camellia bushes in bloom at Aunt Maude's. The bowl will be perfect to float camellias in. She buys the bowl and has it gift wrapped, then she and Virginia step back onto the Lawrenceville sidewalks and head home.

## Chapter Twenty-Four
*Sunday, December 2, 1962*

Ree is headed to Aunt Maude's home today. Today is the annual tour of homes and Aunt Maude's place is at the top of the list. The haughty antebellum home with six columns rising to the second-floor roof is painted a crisp white, with green shutters that are so dark they appear to be black from a distance.

Ree walks up the paved brick walkway and stands in line on the porch to greet Aunt Maude. When it is her turn, she hands Aunt Maude the glass bowl. "This is a bowl to float some of your beautiful camellias in," says Ree, kissing Aunt Maude on the cheek.

"Thank you, dear. I know just the place for it. Isn't this the most exciting day? I can hardly wait for open house every year. My favorite day of the year."

"Yes, it's exciting. Your open house always is, Aunt Maude. You know it is the highlight of the season," says Ree.

"Oh, go on with you, Reeda. Now, go on in and speak to everyone, but I want a moment with you to myself before you go."

"Yes, Aunt Maude. We'll do that."

Ree walks in the front door and passes over flooring with inlaid oak and mahogany. She's stepping back to a time of elegance and tradition. The main hall has two Christmas trees, one on each side of the hall. The towering trees are decorated with glass balls and small lit candles. Ree's guess is that the trees are twelve-feet high. *Only Aunt Maude.*

Further down, the hall is flanked on both sides by large, stunning secretaries. Next to the secretaries are wrought iron stands holding tall, lit candles surrounded by shiny magnolia leaves.

Ree takes it all in. She is proud of Aunt Maude, who lost her husband, Owen, last year at Christmastime. This does not stop Maude from sharing her home and her love of the season. Ree thinks Aunt Maude may imagine Owen here with her today.

After walking through all four rooms decorated for the open house, chatting along the way with the good people of Lawrenceville, Ree walks in to the side yard with its maze of boxwoods. Ree has never walked the maze, but it fascinates her. She is tempted to try it today and has taken her first step when she hears Aunt Maude summoning her.

"Reeda, I am so glad I found you all by yourself. How is everyone in the family?"

"We are thriving, for the most part, but I worry about Daddy."

"Yes, I can see that. This Christmas is hard for me, losing Owen last year and all. I can't imagine how hard it is for James with Mildred murdered, plus he lost Richard, too."

"You know the worst part, Aunt Maude? We still don't know who murdered Mother. Hardly a day goes by that I don't think about it. I do know Uncle Richard didn't murder her."

"You are right, there. I totally agree. By the way, I told you about Owen seeing Richard at Point Clear, didn't I?"

Ree stands very still.

"Ree, I told you, didn't I?"

"No, Aunt Maude, you didn't."

"Well, I must have told James. I know I told someone. Richard was in Point Clear for a conference. This was back in '47. At the Grand Hotel, if I remember correctly. Owen saw Richard—he swore it was Richard—across the lobby, and he was with a lady. By the time Owen crossed the lobby, the two had disappeared."

"That's astounding," says Ree.

"Well, now I've told you. I don't know what to make of it. better get back to my guests. Are you staying, Reeda?"

"No, I have to run. Stuff to do at home. Thank you for bringing Christmas to Lawrenceville in high fashion as always, Aunt Maude." Ree kisses her aunt on the cheek and walks away, leaving the maze for another day.

## Chapter Twenty-Five
*Saturday, December 8, 1962*

James, Virginia, and Ree are on their way to Marion, Alabama. One of the postcards had been mailed from this small town in 1958, just four years earlier. They will be staying with Mason's Uncle Will and Will's wife, Amanda.

"Now, tell me again where we're staying, Reeda," says James.

"On Callander land. At Will Jones' house. It's a long story, so interrupt me when you don't understand something or someone," says Ree. "I'll fill you in."

"These are Dad's relatives, right?" says Virginia.

"Right. As I said, we are staying with Will and Amanda Jones. Will is your father's uncle, Virginia."

"But what is Callander land?" asks Virginia.

"Hang on. Will's first wife was Charlene Callander, daughter of David Henry Callander, who owns a farm near Marion—a 1,200-acre farm to be precise. Will's house is on the farm. I met David Henry Callander once. He is a tower of a man, and he's very impressive. I was only around for a short period of time, but I came to respect him highly."

"And we'll get to meet this Mr. Callander?" asks Virginia.

"Yes, I can almost assure you that you will," says Ree.

"Amanda is Will's second wife?" asks James.

"Yes, Charlene died. Years later, Will married Amanda. Oh, and I haven't mentioned Zia. She is David Henry's daughter. She married David Fotos, who, at one time, owned a sugarcane plantation in Cuba. David and Zia both had harrowing escapes from Cuba."

"And they live on Callander land, too?" asks James.

"Yes, at the large house where David Henry lives," says Ree.

"But none of these people have anything to do with the postcard?" asks Virginia.

"No, we are going to Judson College in Marion for that. You'll see."

\* \* \*

Pulling up in front of Judson's main campus, Ree and family climb out of the car and stand on the sidewalk, confronted by an impressive brick building set on a knoll.

This must be Jewett Hall, the major academic building on campus. It is fashioned after the Governor's Palace in Williamsburg, Virginia, and is topped with a three-storied bell tower identical to the one in Virginia. The Carnegie library, an impressive two-story brick building in its own right, stood to the left of Jewett Hall and the president's home to the right. *Very impressive. And academic.*

Entering Jewett Hall, Ree and the others are met with a student volunteer who escorts them to the president's office. President Anderson stands up from behind his desk and greets them. Introductions are made and the Judson College president invites them to join him at a conference table. They were fortunate he was available to meet them and speak for a few moments.

"Now, what brings you to Judson College?" he asks.

Ree explains the mystery of the blank postcards that come every Christmas.

"And one came from Marion, Alabama, with Jewett Hall on the front in 1958," says James.

"Do you remember if a Richard Todd visited your campus in 1958?" asks Ree.

"No, but my secretary should be able to locate a list of guest lecturers for that year, if that is what he was," he offers.

"Thank you. It's a good place to start," says Ree.

President Anderson leaves the room for a few minutes and returns with a stack of papers in his hands. He sits behind his desk and looks through a list of names on the first sheet.

"Richard Todd, did you say?" says the President.

"Yes," replies James.

"No, but we did have a Charlotte Todd speak about her new book in December of 1958."

President Anderson reaches behind him and pulls a book from the bookshelves.

"Here it is. A signed copy." He hands the book to James.

James turns to the back book cover flap to read Charlotte Todd's biographical information.

"Look. She lives with her husband in Asheville. She teaches history at the University of North Carolina in Asheville. She and her husband served with the Civil Defense in Denver throughout World War II."

James hands the book to Ree who turns it over to stare at the face of a blonde lady with a heart-shaped face, her hair pulled straight back to reveal a face with no wrinkles, although Ree is sure she is in her fifties in the photograph.

"Does this help?" asks President Anderson.

"You have no idea," says Ree.

"This will go a long way in helping us solve our mystery," says James as he stands to shake President Anderson's hand. James and Ree thank him for his time and leave Jewett Hall.

Once outside, Virginia says, "Isn't this amazing? Do you think she was married to your brother, grandfather?"

"I'm just not sure," says James.

"I think it's likely," says Ree. "Aunt Maude just told me last Sunday that Uncle Owen saw Uncle Richard once with a lady at the Grand Hotel. At least the man looked like Richard. Maybe that lady was Charlotte?"

"This is so exciting. When do we go to Asheville?" asks Virginia.

Ree laughs. "I think we'll go. But not tomorrow."

As they get in the car, Ree says, "Now it's time to head to Callander."

\* \* \*

Dinner conversation around the dining room table at Callander is lively. They enjoy a delicious dinner, prepared to perfection, as Ree and her family warm to Mason's relatives.

"You knew my father?" Virginia asks this of Will.

"Of course. He loved to come here to the farm," says Will. "I'll never forget his one and only experience picking cotton. I thought he'd last a few minutes, but my nephew fooled me. Mason stayed with the pickers all day. He was only around thirteen, but he wouldn't give up. That boy was so tired. I thought I'd have to pick him up and carry him to bed. I admired your father immensely, Virginia."

Virginia looks at Ree with that exhilarated look she gets when she hears something special about her father.

"One more thing," says Will. "I would know you are Mason's child if I saw you on the street. You are the spitting image of him." Turning to Ree, Will asks, "Does she have that persistent streak, like Mason?"

"In spades," says Ree, hugging Virginia as she says it.

It's David Henry's turn. "Reeda, I understand you are a journalist. Have you heard about Zia's exploits?"

Ree looks at Zia, and sees a striking lady with a flawless complexion, long black hair pulled back tight in a French twist and pearls in her ears. Ree senses the keen intelligence behind her deep brown eyes.

"I understand you are a journalist. So am I," says Zia to Ree.

"Yes, I write for our local newspaper in Lawrenceville," says Ree.

"You love it, don't you? I sense that about you," says Zia.

"It shows?" says Ree.

"I think so. Tell me about some of your stories."

"My favorite to date is a story about the Cuban Missile Crisis from a Lawrenceville perspective. How it impacts our citizens from the need to store water to adjusting to postponed weddings to worry over sons and daughters in the military."

"I'd love to read that story, Ree. May I call you Ree?"

"Please do. I prefer it," says Ree

"Zia was a reporter for CBS. She went to Cuba to cover a story during the days of Batista. While there, she met David, who owned a sugarcane plantation. They fell in love," says David Henry.

Reeda looks at David with his slicked back hair and tan, handsome face—a face anyone would look at twice.

"Of course I fell in love. Who wouldn't love this fiery, dominating woman?" says David. "No other person could make me leave Cuba."

Zia reaches over and takes David's hand. "We lived in Havana until Castro came into power," she says. "Castro imprisoned both David and me, though at different times. He and my niece, Ellen—she is also a journalist—got me out of Cuba. David was imprisoned for getting me out, but he escaped also."

Speaking for the first time, James turns to David. "It must have been horrible to leave a country you obviously love, a country that was home," he says. "How did you survive it?"

"I have no family in Cuba. My family is here. But it hurts to see my country changed so," says David.

"And the Cuban Missile Crisis. Were you torn?" asks James.

"Of course. It was horrid," says David. "Despite my hatred of the present administration, my heart breaks to think of my Cuba destroyed."

"Ree, you especially will be interested in this rumor David picked up from a Cuban source," says Zia.

"That story is not verified," David quickly interjects.

"Ree will understand. Never report a story without two credible sources. But it's so interesting. I'd love to mention it," says Zia.

"Fine, as long as we remember it's a rumor."

Zia slides to the edge of her chair. "Soviet submarines were almost to Cuba when there was an encounter between American anti-submarine ship and planes and Soviet submarines. Thinking the war had started, the captain of the Soviet submarine ordered a nuclear missile to be fired. The chief of staff ordered the crew to stand down and not fire the missile, but to await orders from the Soviet Union."

"Wow. That one incident would have started a nuclear war. What a fascinating story," says Ree. "I hope one day we'll learn the whole story."

"Yes," says David. "Thank goodness it turned out okay. That is, if the story is true."

"Yes," says Ree.

Turning to look at Virginia, Ree sees a very sleepy daughter.

James notices this too and says, "I think we've got one almost down for the count. With your permission, we need to get Virginia to bed."

Rising from his chair, David Henry says, "We have enjoyed this time with you. I can see why Mason married you, Reeda. You and your family are welcome here any time."

Ree walks over and hugs David Henry. "Thank you for having us, and I want you to promise to give us a tour of Callander the next time we visit."

"You know I'd love to do that," says David Henry.

"And don't forget to send me your article on the Cuban Missile Crisis," says Zia.

"Promise," says Ree, as she walks over to hug David and Zia.

"I, for one, would love that tour," says James as he shakes hands with David Henry.

"I have an idea," says David Henry. "Will, what do you think about them coming for a week this summer?"

"Answering for Will, I think that's a great idea," says Amanda. Will nods his approval.

"So," says Ree, "We'll see you this summer."

Smiling, David Henry says, "Let's make it the middle of July."

"I'm sure that will work for us," says Ree.

"It's on the Callander calendar," says David Henry. He laughs aloud at his own pun.

## Chapter Twenty-Six
*Wednesday, December 12, 1962*

Wednesday night of the following week finds Ree and Harold walking down Perry Street in the direction of the Colonial. It and the drive-in are the two movie theaters in town. The front of the orangish stone theater features a ticket booth. Large glass cases nearby display the latest movie posters. Tonight, there are posters for *Gypsy* with Rosalind Russell and Natalie Wood, which is showing now, and for *Taras Bulba* and *To Kill a Mockingbird*, both coming in a few weeks.

Ree stops in front of the *To Kill a Mockingbird* poster. "I can't wait to see this one. It comes out Christmas Day," she says.

"Me, too," says Harold. "If it is half as good as the book, it is a winner."

"*To Kill a Mockingbird* is on my top ten list of books. You know, Harper Lee's father was a lawyer. Do you think he was the inspiration for Atticus Finch?"

"I don't know, but it's one of my favorites, too."

Harold buys the tickets. Bypassing the popcorn, he and Ree walk into the theater. They pass all the teenage couples on the back two rows who will no doubt neck during the entire movie.

Ree looks up at Harold. "I better not ever find Virginia necking in this or any other theater."

"Oh, really?" says Harold. "Tell me you never sat with a boy in the back row."

Ree laughs. "Okay, you have me there. But Virginia won't."

It's Harold's turn to laugh. "We'll see about that."

Ree and Harold both laugh at the Bugs Bunny cartoon that plays before the movie. They sit ever so close, mesmerized as the reluctant Louise blossoms into Gypsy Rose Lee. But what a sad story of a mother who tried to live through her daughters. They walk silently out of the theater until Harold breaks out in his own version of "Everything's Coming Up Roses."

\* \* \*

After kissing Harold on the front porch, Ree walks into her home to find James standing in the kitchen.

"There's a letter for you over on the counter," says James. "Oh, and did you and Harold have a good time?"

It's an innocent question. One any parent would ask an older daughter. For some reason, Ree finds herself blushing.

"Yes, Dad, we had a good time," says Ree. She walks to the counter and picks up the letter. *Strange.* She notices the childlike printing of her address on the front of the letter. There is no return address. Opening the letter, Ree finds the same child-like printing inside the envelope, but there is nothing remotely child-like about the content.

**Stop trying to find your mother's killer.**
**You may be next.**

Ree's eyes blink—her only movement as she stands very still, holding the letter in her right hand.

"Reeda, are you all right?" asks James.

Ree comes to life, stuffs the letter back in its envelope, and says, "Yes, Dad. Just a letter from an old college friend."

"I am glad you had a good time tonight, Reeda. I like your Harold a lot."

"Yes, Dad, I think I do, too."

## Chapter Twenty-Seven
*Thursday, December 13, 1962*

Ree kneels beside Mason's grave at the end of her work day the following afternoon. Once, just after his death, Ree could place her hands on Mason's grave and feel his presence. But not so much now. Just the quietness of the old historic cemetery. But the love is still there—the love she feels for Mason and for their life together.

Ree tells Mason about the trip to Marion, complete with lengthy tales of all the Callander people. The stories unravel a little at a time. She reminds him about picking cotton as a boy and tells him how David Henry swears Virginia is the spitting image of Mason. She smiles when she shares that they are invited back this summer.

Then she tells Mason about the letter she received. She admits she is a little afraid. Just as she does, she hears the sharp snap of a branch in the wooded cemetery. It is unsettling. Looking around, she sees no one.

Picking up a smooth stone, she kisses it and places it on Mason's tombstone, just as she had a week before.

* * *

Ree walks into the kitchen to find Gus and her father deep in conversation. Gus is telling James about the time he was principal at Central Gwinnett High School, of course. His students scored higher on the SAT and he had more advanced placement students enrolled at that time than Central does now. James is trying to hide the fact he wants to scream.

"Well, hello you two. You know, Gus, I heard you had the largest Beta Club in the state right here at Central Gwinnett when you were principal," says Ree.

Gus beams. James bites on his fist to hold back that scream.

"What are you two up to?" asks Ree.

"We are going to the church to get the luminary ready to set out the around square. Gus is helping this year," says James.

Ree's face lights up with a smile. "Oh, it's not long before Christmas Eve," says Ree. "I'm so excited."

James sets the white paper bags, each one weighted with sand, on the kitchen counter. Each contains lit candles. Gus and James will place the bags all around the square on Christmas Eve, and the candles burn through the night in a celebration of the coming of the Christ Child. It is a labor of love for James and is one of the Lawrenceville Christmas traditions Ree treasures most.

Ree helps James put on his coat and hugs him. "You two be careful. Great to see you, Gus," says Ree, as she walks them to the front door.

Glancing into the front parlor, Ree see the postcards set out on the coffee table. She remembers the Judson discussion about the lady who worked in Denver with her husband during World War II. Ree walks over and fans out the postcards, studying them one by one. Five postcards, dated from 1941 through 1945, are postmarked Denver. Ree has chills. She can hardly wait to track down this Charlotte Todd.

## Chapter Twenty-Eight
*Friday, December 14, 1962*

Ree has taken the morning off to Christmas shop around the Lawrenceville Square. She knows she will buy James a book when she and Virginia go to Rich's in downtown Atlanta tomorrow. She has already purchased a dark green wool cardigan at Alford's for her father and is now in McConnell's Five and Dime on Perry Street, looking for an idea that's just right for Virginia.

Walking down the aisles searching for inspiration, Ree spots a Pat Boone record tote with a dreamy-looking teen girl and a record player on the front cover. A caricature of Pat Boone is on the cover, too. Ree knows Virginia loves Pat Boone's songs—especially "Love Letters in the Sand"—because she walks through the house singing it all the time. *Good grief! So annoying.*

A record player and this tote. What a great gift for Virginia. She will love them.

Thrilled with her purchase, Ree walks out of McConnell's and is heading toward Wilson's when she runs into Dennis. Literally.

"Oh, my gosh. I am so sorry for running into you, Dennis. I didn't see you."

"That is no problem," says Dennis.

"Well, you have a good day."

Ignoring her comment, Dennis says, "I bought Christmas lights at Wilson's to put around the circulation desk. I love Christmas."

"That is a great idea. I'll have to come in to see your lights," says Ree.

Dennis gets that glazed look in his eyes. He stands very still.

Ree shrugs and walks away. She hears Dennis say, "I loved your mother. She shouldn't have done what she did."

Chills run up and down Ree's arms. *What a strange thing to say.* Even for Dennis, it's strange. Ree watches Dennis lumber away.

Ree is meeting Harold for lunch at Edge's. She has just enough time to look for a Christmas gift for Aunt Maude in Wilson's before she meets Harold. On the right side of the store she finds glass cases, several filled with Hummel figurines. The porcelain statues, mostly of children, are enormously popular—and expensive. Ree has always wanted one, but can't afford it.

She spots four crystal ice-cream bowls with footed pedestals. They scream Aunt Maude. She has them wrapped in glossy Christmas paper covered with green reindeers, then rushes out of the store to meet Harold.

\*\*\*

Harold stands to greet Ree as she enters Edge's. He pulls out a chair for her to sit down.

"I'm sorry I'm late. I was Christmas shopping on the square," says Ree.

"You are not late. You are perfect," says Harold.

"Good grief," says Ree.

After they both order—no need to look at the menu—Ree says, "So, what do you want for Christmas?"

Harold doesn't even stop to think. "I want that Ray Charles album of country music. I have heard a few of the tracks from the album and love it. Who would think Ray Charles would sing country? Your turn. What do you want?"

"I want you to help me spread the last of Aunt Clarisse's ashes. That's all. I need to put her to rest… all of her." Ree says this emphatically, without smiling.

*Unusual,* Harold thinks. Ree usually finds Aunt Clarisse's ashes amusing, especially since the rosebush episode. "I think I can do that." Harold pauses, then asks, "Are you all right? You seem off somehow."

Ree slumps in her chair. She tears up.

"Okay, you are scaring me. What is wrong?"

Ree is embarrassed. She hates to be emotional in public. She wipes her eyes with the knuckles of her right hand and

## The December Postcards

decides to tell Harold about the note. She takes the letter out of her purse and hands it to him.

Harold looks at the child-like printing on the front of the envelope before him and frowns. He pulls the letter out, reads it, looks at her, and explodes with fury and concern.

"What the hell, Ree? You are being threatened?"

Ree nods.

Harold reaches across the table and takes both her hands in his. He says, "Over my dead body. That's what it'll take for anyone to hurt you."

Ree is touched. She smiles at Harold. What a knight in shining armor.

"I mean it, Ree. You have to take this seriously." Harold, frowning, sits and thinks for a minute. "This is the way it's going to be. If you are walking home after dark, I will be there to walk you home. If I can't, James will. I think you will be okay walking around the square in the daylight, but you are not going anywhere alone at night. I'm serious, Ree."

Ree doesn't react to Harold. No way is she going to have someone following her around everywhere she goes.

"And another thing," he says. "You have to show this letter to James. He has to know what's going on. You know he will want to protect you."

Ree reaches for Harold's hands. Squeezing them, she thanks him for caring about her.

"Well, of course I care about you. You are my girl. Now, put a smile on your face and let's walk out of here. We are already feeding the gossip mill enough. Here we go, sweetheart. Let's go."

## Chapter Twenty-Nine
*Saturday, December 15, 1962*

*It's the Pink Pig!*

A pink steel pig named Priscilla loops around a monorail on the rooftop of Rich's department store in downtown Atlanta. With its smiling pig's face painted on front of the first car and a curly tale attached to the last car, the Pink Pig is a favorite Christmas tradition for children all over the South. They flock to Atlanta to ride the one-of-a-kind train and Christmas shop with their parents.

Feeling child-like herself, Ree hops on the Pink Pig with Virginia. *Look at the Atlanta stores from up here.* From here, they can look down on the Christmas Village and see the seventy-foot Christmas tree on top of Rich's glass bridge. Virginia squeals with delight. Ree stores this memory in her heart.

Getting off the ride, Ree and Virginia get a pink pig sticker that says, of course, "I rode the pink pig at Rich's."

Next the two are off to the bookstore to get a book for James. What is it about a bookstore? The smell of chemicals and ink swirl together to create a smell of freshness that fills your nostrils when you open a freshly printed book. And then there is the satisfying sight of an array of colorful covers. All those books lined up on shelves and just waiting to be opened

Ree picks up and puts down *Seven Days in May* by two authors, Fletcher Knebel and Charles W. Bailey II. She peruses *Fail-Safe*, the bestseller by another author duo, Eugene Burdick and Harvey Wheeler, then takes a look at *A Shade of Difference* by Allen Drury. Finally, she picks up *Youngblood Hawke* by Herman Wouk.

This is the one, she thinks. James will love this story of an aspiring young author in New York. And the novel is written by the author of Pulitzer-Prize Winner *The Caine Mutiny*.

Ree tucks the book under her arm and heads for the record department. She notices the most popular albums displayed on the wall to her left. *Modern Sounds in Country and Western Music* by Ray Charles is featured prominently.

"Let's listen to this album, Virginia. It's what Harold wants for Christmas. I want to see what makes it so special."

Ree finds the album in one of the many record bins and takes it to the cashier. She has to give her driver's license to the cashier in order to take the album into one of the glass-enclosed listening booths that line the right wall of the store. Once in the booth, Ree takes the album out of its cover and places it carefully on the record player. She and Virginia listen to "You Don't Know Me," "Bye Bye Love," and "I Can't Stop Loving You."

"I like it, Mom," says Virginia.

Smiling, Ree says, "I do, too." She places the album back in its cover and says, "That does it. We're through buying gifts."

Quietly, Virginia says, "No, we're not."

"We're not? Who did we miss?"

"Bill," says Virginia.

"Oh. Really?"

"Sam told me Bill is buying me a Christmas gift. I want to buy him one, too."

"Of course, you do. Any ideas?"

"I know he likes "Return to Sender" by Elvis. He sings it all the time. While we're here, I could buy him the 45."

"He doesn't have it?"

"No, Sam told me he wants it and other records for Christmas."

"Then, I think it's perfect. Let's grab a copy, get my license back, and buy these."

With their purchase complete, Ree stretches her arms high in the air and waves her hands.

"What are you doing besides embarrassing me?" asks Virginia.

"I'm celebrating. Christmas shopping is done. Let's go home."

## Chapter Thirty
*Tuesday, December 18, 1962*

Ree is listening with one ear tuned to WLAW as she gets ready for work. A show entitled *Who Did It?* airs every Tuesday after Johnnie Day's morning show. Retired Deputy Sheriff Stanley Butts produces the show locally. The majority of his shows are about unsolved crimes in this area.

The name Billy Faucett catches her attention. Now she is listening with both ears pealed to the radio. Deputy Butts is discussing the murders in 1936 and 1937—the ones Ree had discovered in the back issues of the *News-Herald*. He moves on to discuss a murder in Lawrenceville, also in 1937. The murder of Joy Harris, a local sharecropper's wife, by blunt instrument. Allegedly a crime committed by Faucett.

Ree sits down slowly. *Billy Faucett murdered someone here in Lawrenceville? Was this reported in the* News-Herald?

Ree has always questioned whether Billy Faucett, the infamous serial murderer, could have murdered her mother.

Deputy Butts goes on to say the husband of Joy Harris resolved to find Billy Faucett. Joy was survived by a son, Troy Harris, who lives locally to this day. Deputy Butts asks for anyone listening who knows anything about the murders by Billy Faucett to please write him at WLAW, 829 Crogan St. Northeast, Lawrenceville.

Ree is energized. She can hardly wait to finish her articles at the *News-Herald* and look for the Joy Harris story in the archives.

\* \* \*

Seeing Ree walking up Perry, Miss Birdie comes out of Cato's to chat. "I tell you, Reeda, that Harold Perry sure is a happy man these days."

Ree hugs Miss Birdie carefully as to not disturb the coiffured bird's nest on Miss Birdie's head. "You know, Miss Birdie, I've noticed that about Harold. I think he is a happy man."

Miss Birdie whoops. "I knew it. I just knew it. Harold Perry is the man for you."

Ree says goodbye to Miss Birdie as she heads toward the *News-Herald* building. Pleased to see Miss Betty on the phone with a customer, Ree sneaks by her and heads to her desk.

She has three stories to write before she leaves for the day. The Central Gwinnett Band story delights her. There is a concert this Friday, December 21$^{st}$, at eight o'clock. The band is directed by Mr. Leon Clem. Apparently, there is a shortage of instruments and most students cannot afford one, so there are students who can't join the band because of their inability to obtain an instrument. The school is asking that anyone in the town who has instruments they are willing to donate to please bring them to the principal's office at Central Gwinnett. Mayor Holt has declared this week, December 13 through December 21, to be Band Week.

Christmas is the best season for human interest stories. The Salvation Army, working with the Metropolitan Atlanta United Appeal, has gifted more funds for the needy in Gwinnett than ever before. Christmas giving was organized by the Welfare Department.

Unrelated to the Christmas season, the Lawrenceville Jaycees conducted a vehicle check on December 8. Of the 189 vehicles checked, 156 were not safe. Only nine cars had seatbelts. Completing the Jaycee story first, Ree turns her attention to the more uplifting stories and places all three on Mr. Monroe's desk.

She heads for the storage room to look through the leather-bound books that hold Lawrenceville's history. She pulls out the book containing the newspapers dated 1937, places it on the table, and begins her search.

*Here it is.* Joy Harris, wife of sharecropper Dan Harris, had been found murdered in the field behind her house. A blow to her head killed her. She was found by her son, Troy. The article goes on to mention Dan Harris who sharecrops on Mr. Winston's farm, which is located off the Dacula Highway.

Ree closes the book and just sits, thinking. *So horrible.* Three unsolved cases of women who were brutally murdered. Four counting her mother. Ree feels the same pain she always feels when she thinks about her mother's death. The pain and the longing. Longing for the warmth and love her mother brought to her young life.

Ree puts the book back on the shelf and gathers her things. Time to go home.

\* \* \*

One more thing she must do today. Ree needs to contact Charlotte, the lady in Asheville associated with Richard. Could she have been Richard's wife? Ree remembers she taught at University of North Carolina Asheville. A good place to start.

Picking up the phone, Ree dials "0" to get the operator. Thank goodness this operator is a patient one. Ree explains she needs to contact a Charlotte Todd in the history department at the University of North Carolina Asheville.

After a brief pause, the operator comes back on the line to tell Ree she found a telephone number for the chair of the department. Would Ree like that number?

Ree sucks in her breath and dials.

"Charlotte Todd, history department."

For a moment, Ree can't speak.

"Hello, is anyone there?"

What does she say? She hasn't thought it through. She just blurts out, "I am Reeda Jones, and I think you knew my uncle, Richard Todd Martin."

Silence on the other end of the line. Ree is about to hang up when Charlotte replies, "Yes, Richard and I were married. I know who you are, Reeda. I know all about James and the family and Lawrenceville."

Ree begins to cry.

"I hope you know how much Richard loved all of you," Charlotte says. There is a softness in her voice. "I think you know he was an amazing man. And it hurts me to tell you he passed away last year."

"No postcard," says Ree.

"Yes, that's right. I would love to meet with you and James, assuming James is still alive."

"Yes, my father is very much alive. And he has never stopped mourning Richard."

"Would it be possible for you and your family to visit Asheville?"

"Yes, I'd like that. I'm sure Dad would, too."

"Are you married? Would you bring your husband?"

"My husband, Mason, died in 1950. We have a daughter, Virginia. She will be so excited to visit."

"I can hardly wait for you to come. Please, stay with me. I am rattling around in this big old five-bedroom house and would love the company."

"Are you sure?"

"Of course, I'm sure. Now, when can you come? Please tell me you can come before the end of the year. How about Saturday, the 29th? Is that too soon?"

Ree laughs. She is delighted with Charlotte Todd. "I tell you my heart is racing. I am so excited to have found you. Yes, the 29th will work. We will make it work."

"I am excited, too. I look forward to sharing Richard with you and your sharing Richard with me. What a wonderful Christmas gift."

"I couldn't agree more," says Ree. "Please have a merry Christmas, and we will be in touch. May we call you on Christmas Day?"

"Of course. I'll send a Christmas card today with a number where you can reach me. And my address. I will probably be at my cousin's home on Christmas day, but please call me there. I'll include her number, too."

"Our address is 125 North Clayton Street in Lawrenceville, Georgia. I look forward to your card. I thank God we found you, Charlotte. You are the perfect Christmas gift for our family."

"I feel the same," says Charlotte. "See you on the 29th."

Ree hangs up the telephone and thinks of James. He will be devastated to know his suspicions are true about Richard, but he will be thankful for Charlotte. A miraculous Christmas gift.

## Chapter Thirty-One
*Monday, December 24, 1962*

Christmas Eve already. Ree looks around the room as she puts on her coat for the Christmas Eve service at the church. A lovely warmth spreads through her as she watches James and Gus argue. Virginia looks under the tree for Bill's gift. She'll give it to him after the service. And Harold is here too. He is staring at her with a look that shows love—love for her, Reeda.

They walk out the front door and stop. All around the Lawrenceville Square she sees James' luminary, the warm candlelight shining through the white paper bags. So beautiful! A Christmas gift from James to Lawrenceville. Ree reaches for Harold's hand as they make the turn on the corner and head toward the church.

Once inside, they sit behind the senator and Delia. The senator stands up to shake hands all around. He wishes James and Gus a Merry Christmas and mentions to Ree that he remembers all the Christmas plays her mother directed through the years. Ree loves the memory that comes to her mind. She thanks the senator. Maybe he does have a human side.

The principal from Central High comes up to speak to James and Gus. He thanks Gus for his volunteer work at the high school. Gus beams. "I see you have been running laps at the track," the principal says to Gus.

"Yes, got to keep in shape," says Gus.

In an aside to James, who is sitting at the end of the row, the principal says, "Can you please tell him to stop criticizing all the students when he's on the track? They are complaining."

"I'll try. You know he still thinks he is the principal," says James.

"How well I know. Merry Christmas to you and yours," he says.

"And to you and the family," says James, patting him on the back.

Ree looks around the church. Her eyes rest on the Christmas tree in the front of the church with its Chrismon ornaments displaying the symbols of Christ. Then she sees the windows decorated with candles and magnolia leaves, the ladies in their finest dresses and gloves, and the men is suits and bright white shirts.

You can feel the love in the air, Ree thinks. That Christmas feeling. There is nothing quite like it. Ree feels it when the first wreaths hang on the doors of stores around the square and again when the tree on the courthouse lawn is lit on Thanksgiving night. It is the most intense feeling of pure love, and Ree knows it comes from Christ. She knows it's up to you to spread it—that love from Christ.

After the service, Gus and James walk Miss Gladys home. She had been waiting outside the church and made it obvious she wanted an escort home. James and Gus humbly obliged.

Jim Anderson walks up with Bill and asks if Virginia could come home with them for cake and ice cream. Bill's father promises he will walk Virginia home himself afterwards, and she'll only be gone an hour. Ree looks at the expression on Virginia's face—the face of a cute puppy begging for her to say yes. Ree thanks him for the invite and watches her daughter walk away, her first gift for a boy tucked in her bag.

"Just like I like it. It's just you and me," says Harold.

Ree takes his arm as they walk home. After they hang up their coats and brew fresh coffee, they sit around the tree. Ree bends and picks up Harold's gift.

"I have a gift for you, Harold." She hands Harold the flat gift wrapped in red, green, and yellow glossy paper and topped with a large, fluffy, red bow.

There are gift receivers who rip the ribbon and paper off to get the gift and there are those who carefully remove bows or ribbons. They run their fingers under the tape, so as to not tear the paper. They fold the paper for future use. Harold is the latter.

Ree is ready to scream, "Open the darn gift," when he finally pulls the record from its wrapping.

"Ray Charles! I love this one," says Harold. "I think my favorite is 'I Can't Stop Loving You.'" He turns to her. "It's true, Ree. I can't stop loving you."

Ree tears up.

"Now, no tears, Reeda." Harold walks over to his coat and pulls out a box with Santa wrapping paper and a red pompom bow on top. He hands it to Ree.

Ree removes the bow. From the box she removes a polished wooden box with a top painted with a full moon and a weeping willow tree. The box top has a chip and some flaking paint. To Ree, it is beautiful.

"Open it," says Harold.

Ree opens the box to find an oval silver locket. "It's beautiful, Harold."

"It was my great grandmother's. Given to her by my great grandfather. Our family custom is that the men give the locket to the lady they love. If the lady loves him back, she will keep the locket and fill it with their pictures."

Ree faces Harold, puts her arms around his neck, and kisses him. No words needed.

## Chapter Thirty-Two
*Thursday, December 27, 1962*

Ree is in Sheriff Pitts' office. She just caught him as he was locking up for an early lunch and apologizes for interrupting.

"No worries," says Sheriff Pitts. "Come in, Reeda. Sit down."

All of a sudden loud banging—metal on metal—reverberates down the hall. "Whatever is that?" asks Ree, startled.

"It's the superintendent's office. When a call comes in, the secretary answers it. If the call is for the superintendent, the secretary bangs on the radiator. That's his signal to pick up."

"Oh," says Ree.

The sheriff smiles.

Recovering, Ree says, "Sheriff, I'll make this quick. Do you remember the Harris murder? In 1937? She may have been one of the victims of Billy Faucett.

"Not right off hand. Remember Sheriff Croft was sheriff then. I'll check the files though."

Sheriff Pitts leaves the room and returns with a folder containing only a few pieces of paper in it. One of the papers has the name of the deceased, Joy Harris, written in pencil in rather sloppy handwriting. The deceased husband's name, Dan Harris, and the name of their son, Troy Harris, are listed just below the name of the murder victim. The last entry on the page is the address of Mr. Winston's farm on the Dacula Highway where Dan Harris had been a sharecropper. Also included in the folder is a yellowed copy of the news article Ree read in the *News-Herald*.

"I see no evidence the Harris murder was investigated. I wouldn't put it past Sheriff Croft to put this case aside in favor of investigating the murders of the more well-known persons."

Ree remembers the thick file containing information on her mother's murder. "You mean it was beneath him to investigate the murder of a sharecropper's wife?"

"It wouldn't surprise me. Sheriff Croft was a disgrace to the office," says Sheriff Pitts.

"I feel so sorry for Mr. Harris and the son. Do you know the son?" Ree asks.

"Sure. Troy. He still has a farm on Dacula Highway near the Winston farm. Calls it the Harris Land. It's written on the mailbox. I know he has a family—two sons if I remember right—and a wife, Alice, who bakes the best blackberry cobbler you ever tasted. They pretty much keep to themselves except for church. I go to church with them. That's how I know."

Ree looks at her watch. She knows where the Winston farm is. The Harris farm shouldn't be hard to find. If she skips lunch, she should be able to go and get back to the *News-Herald* by the end of her lunch period.

Thanking Sheriff Pitts, Ree leaves his office, gets in her car, and heads in the direction of Dacula Highway. She's right. The Harris farm is not hard to find. It's right past Winston's farm on the right. The mailbox with "Harris Land" written on it is obvious.

Ree pulls in the driveway and approaches a white clapboard house with a small but pleasing front porch and dark blue shutters flanking the windows on the front of the house. Rocking chairs line the front porch, and a man about Ree's age is sitting in the chair closest to the front door. He rises when Ree gets out of her car and starts up the brick walk.

He's friendly, this man wearing overalls and looking comfortable in his skin. Ree notices the dirt under his nails, indicating he farms the land, and the furrows on his face, likely caused by long hours in the hot sun.

"Hello, Mrs. Jones," says the man. Ree assumes he is Troy Harris.

"But how did you…?"

"The sheriff called me. Figured you'd be heading my way sooner than later."

"Oh," says Ree.

"The sheriff says you lost your mother just like I lost mine. I sure feel sorry for you."

"Thank you," says Ree.

"It never stops hurting, does it?" says Troy.

"No, it never does," says Ree.

They pause and listen to the sound of the breeze in the nearby oak trees.

"I've investigated," says Ree. "Especially Billy Faucett. They think he murdered a lot of women in this area."

"Mrs. Jones, you can stop researching. And don't you worry none about Billy Faucett."

Ree looks at him, brows wrinkling. Trying to understand what Troy is saying.

"Billy Faucett won't be killing any more women."

Ree looks straight in Troy's eyes. He nods.

Ree stands very still. *Good grief. Troy killed Billy Faucett.* She stands frozen for a few minutes more. Ree finally nods back and turns to leave. She's not sure she wants to stay to ask any further questions.

"Mrs. Jones, would you like some of my wife's blackberry cobbler before you go?"

Ree smiles at Troy. "I hear it's wonderful, but if I don't hurry, I'll be late for work."

"Then, you take care. Nice to meet you, Mrs. Jones. I read those articles you write in the paper. I enjoy them."

"Thank you for that, Mr. Harris." Ree pauses. "Thank you for everything."

It's Troy's turn to smile. "You are very welcome, Mrs. Jones."

\* \* \*

After dinner that evening, Ree takes ornaments off the Christmas tree. All the decorations must be down before the new year or you will have bad luck. That's the superstition anyway. Ree is not sure she believes this but doesn't take a chance… *just in case*. It's always sad to see her mother's ornaments go back in the box for another year.

Ree thinks about this Christmas and smiles at the memory of Virginia opening her gift of the record player and Pat Boone records. Virginia actually squealed. Ree realizes she will hear "Love Letters in the Sand" over and over and over, but it's worth it to have seen the joy on Virginia's face.

James loved his book, *Youngblood Hawke*, and he settled down in his chair with the book and an afghan late Christmas afternoon after Gus left for home. Aunt Maude outdid herself with her Lane Cake. What a warm family Christmas. Ree tears up at the memory.

The last thing left to do after finishing the tree is to take down her mother's pictures in the living and dining rooms. As she removes the last picture from the wall, Ree rubs a finger over a nail hole. It will be there, waiting for their next Christmas. What will Ree's world be like then?

## Chapter Thirty-Three
*Saturday, December 29, 1962*

Ree realizes that the tall, elegant lady who answers the door at one of Asheville's old, historic homes is the same lady with blonde hair and a heart-shaped face that Ree, James, and Virginia had first seen on the back of Charlotte's book.

"Oh, you are Reeda, James, and Virginia. I am delighted to see you. Come in. Come in," says Charlotte.

James takes Charlotte's hand in a courtly manner and says, "Thank you for inviting us to your home. I feel I am touching a piece of Richard by being with you."

Tears form in the corners of Charlotte's eyes. "I feel the very same," she says. "But let's don't stand here. Come, let's sit. I've made some fresh lemonade. We can talk. Johnny will bring your luggage in."

As if on cue, a young boy in brown corduroy pants and a plaid shirt that is not buttoned correctly comes down the hall behind them. Ree finds him charming. He has one front tooth missing and a tuft of hair hangs over his forehead, almost to his eyes. "Is this your company, Miss Charlotte?"

"Yes, Johnny. This is Mr. James, Miss Reeda, and Miss Virginia. Could I ask you to bring in their luggage? You know the rooms to put them in."

"Yes ma'am, be glad to," says Johnny.

Charlotte takes them to the kitchen with its twelve-foot ceiling, cherry cabinet, immense gas stove, and a round table that seats ten. "I like to bring my friends to the kitchen instead of one of those stuffy old rooms in the front of the house," says Charlotte. "Now, who wants lemonade?" As she serves the lemonade, she says, as much to herself as to her guests, "Where do we start? I can't begin to know."

"Tell me, what do you know about the time right after Mildred's murder? That would be a good place to start," says James.

"I know Richard was accused of the murder, put in jail, and that you helped him escape."

Not a sound. Shock.

Finally, Ree breaks the silence. "Dad, you let Uncle Richard out of jail?"

James had been slumped over, looking at the floor. At Ree's question, he sits back and looks his daughter in the eye. "Yes, I did. I knew Richard could never kill Mildred. Or anyone else, for that matter. I knew he would never get a fair trial with Sheriff Croft in office. I did what I had to do."

Ree is still shocked. She never once thought her dad had helped Richard escape.

"Another thing," says James. "Richard's cane had been at the Feely House for weeks. I kept meaning to return it to him."

"So, anyone could have used the cane to kill Grandmother?" asks Virginia.

"Absolutely," says James.

Once they recover from the stunning news that her father had helped his brother break out of the Lawrenceville jail, Ree shares their findings with Charlotte and tells her about the trip to Amelia. She recounts how she found Richard Todd's book in a bookstore on the island. Ree tells her about the trip to Tuscaloosa, following the trail of postcards after she discovered that Sheriff Croft would have never given Richard a fair trial in Lawrenceville.

Last, Ree tells Charlotte about their trip to Judson where they had first learned about her—Charlotte Todd. Ree talks about how she came home and matched the Denver postcards to the war years, when Charlotte and Richard had lived in Denver.

"If you had not tracked down the locations where the postcards were mailed, you would never have found me. Thank goodness you did. I should have contacted you when Richard died. I was afraid."

"Yes. It's very miracle-like," says Ree.

## The December Postcards

"Now, I have a question," says James. "The postcards were from all over. Did Richard travel to all those places?"

Charlotte laughed, a pleasant soft laughter. "We traveled to Paris together in 1948 and mailed that postcard while there. What a special time for us. We were so in love. The cards from the South and the ones mailed from Denver were from Richard. I mailed cards from the other European cities and from cities on the West coast. Before you ask, we had friends, even strangers sometimes, address all the postcards. We knew anyone could recognize Richard's writing, so we didn't take any chances there.

"But I just knew the postcards were from Richard. I had to believe he was alive and well. When the postcard did not arrive last Christmas, I was devastated. Still am," says James.

"How did he die?" asks Virginia.

"He had a heart attack. He was sitting in the library in his favorite chair reading a book about the Cherokee Indians that had just arrived through the mail. There was no sound. No cry for help. He was just gone. I stuck my head in the library door to ask him a question and knew right away when I saw him. I knew I had lost my Richard."

"How very horrible for you," says Ree.

James starts to cry. No one knows how long they sit while James cries.

Finally, Charlotte stands up. "But look at us," she says. "We are all together. Richard is here, too. I'm sure he has that crooked smile on his face and love in his heart to see us together. So, we are going to celebrate. Go put your dancing shoes on, as my father used to say when we were going out. We are going to the Grove Park Inn for dinner."

\* \* \*

Ree and the entire family are astonished by the impressive interior of the Grove Park Inn. They are amazed at the large lobby with overstuffed furniture and enormous fireplaces situated at each end of each room. The fireplaces are thirty feet wide and twelve feet tall—large enough for the four of them to stand inside.

As they are being seated in the restaurant, Virginia is still talking about the fireplaces. "We could really stand inside?" she asks.

"Yes, if the logs were removed, we would be very comfortable standing inside," Charlotte says.

"Tell us more about the Inn," James says to Charlotte. "I love the huge rocks used to build the hotel and the fireplaces. Some of them are massive."

"I love Grove Park Inn. Richard and I often came for drinks and dinner. What to tell you? Hmm." Charlotte thinks for a moment, then continues. "One interesting fact is that F. Scott Fitzgerald stayed here in 1935 and 1936. He was recovering from alcohol addiction and was well enough to write in 1936."

"*The Great Gatsby?*" says James.

"No, I believe that was written earlier in his life. I don't know what he wrote while here, but if you find room numbers 441 and 443, you will be standing in front of the rooms where Scott Fitzgerald lived and worked. He slept in one room and wrote in the other."

"I would love to see. The writer in me is stirred by the fact that Fitzgerald wrote here," says Ree.

"Oh, this inn has loads of history. No small number of presidents have stayed here. But enough about Grove Park Inn. Please, tell me about Richard. What was he like growing up? I want to know anything you can tell me," Charlotte says as she turns to James.

"Where to start?" says James. "I can tell you I admired him more than anyone I ever knew. He always took up for the underdog—hated bullies. I remember him taking on the heaviest guy in school because the guy was picking on me. Funny, not one person bothered me after that."

"And his love of history?" asks Charlotte.

"Always there. I remember Richard especially loved stories about the Cherokee and Creek Indians. Once, my father took Richard to search for arrowheads. I had never seen him so excited."

"I love this young Richard. He did not change. When we were traveling, he wanted to stop and read every historic plaque on the highway. What about you, Ree? What do you remember of Richard?"

Ree shares the story of Richard teaching math to the boy who pushed her down. "Terry was his name. He was frustrated with his failure in math and hated me for my success with it. Richard told him he had to come to my house every Saturday for the next four weeks for math lessons or Richard would take him to the sheriff. You know, I believe I heard Terry is teaching math in Forsyth County."

The group laughs out loud about Terry teaching math. Charlotte hugs herself, obviously thrilled to hear about the Richard she didn't know.

"Now, what about you. How did you and Richard meet?" says Ree.

"Now, there's a story. We met in 1937 at a convention on Jekyll Island. Mistakenly, we had both been scheduled to be the key note speaker. Richard graciously stepped aside for me to open the convention. I tracked him down as the convention ended for the day and convinced him the least I could do was buy him dinner. It went from there. The love of my life."

"Oh," says Virginia, obviously relishing the story.

"Now, I recommend Bananas Foster for the adults. The rum sauce is amazing. And ice cream for Virginia?" says Charlotte.

Virginia wrinkles her nose.

"Virginia would love ice-cream," says Ree. "Virginia, I promise you the first bite of my Bananas Foster."

"Wonderful. And then we'll get you home," says Charlotte.

*** 

The next morning, as they finish breakfast, everyone in the group expresses regret that they have so little time left to spend together. Ree and her family have to drive back to Lawrenceville.

Then, Charlotte remembers something odd. Richard and Mildred had an argument about some papers Mildred found at the Feely House. He had told her about it. She retells the story as she recalls it. "I have no idea what the argument was about. Richard didn't say. Evidently, it was unusual for Mildred and him to argue. It upset Richard."

Ree remembers Dennis mentioning an argument between Richard and her mother. Maybe this was the argument he remembered? Something to muse over.

At that point, Charlotte leaves the room for a moment and returns with an urn. It appears to be made from solid brass and has a blue lacquer finish. She hands the urn to James.

James frowns.

"It is Richard, James. I couldn't give all of him to you. I have an urn as well. Richard deserves to be with you, as well as me."

James' hands tremble as he takes the urn from Charlotte. Ree knows what this means to her father, and she knows he will want to grieve in private.

Ree stands up to hug Charlotte. "I know how special this time spent together has been for all of us. It is too special to lose. Now that we have found you, you may not be able to get rid of us. One of us may be calling you every week."

Charlotte quietly says, "I would like that very much."

Virginia asks, "Will you come see us?"

"I would love to come to Lawrenceville."

Not wasting any time, Ree says, "Good. Can you come in January? James has a birthday on January 14."

Charlotte laughs. "I will make that happen, if I can bring Johnny. I don't travel alone these days."

"Of course, bring Johnny," says James.

"It's settled then. It makes it easier to leave, knowing we'll see you soon," says Ree.

Charlotte hugs James and Virginia, holding to each tightly. Then, she steps back and watches them get in their car and start down the drive lined with pyramid-shaped Fraser firs. She watches the road until the car disappears from view.

## Chapter Thirty-Four
*Monday, December 31, 1962*

### New Year's Eve

James and Ree had been up late last night discussing what to do about Richard. Do they put his ashes on a shelf and keep the whole thing a secret? Do they tell Sheriff Pitts? Do they plan a funeral and run a story in the paper?

Definitely not run a story in the paper. Tell Sheriff Pitts, yes. Plan a funeral, yes.

Before going to bed, they had decided they would have a graveyard service. Just a private service. Aunt Maude and Gus will be there plus the three of them. Harold will be there, too. The family has a plot at the historic cemetery—a plot large enough to hold the remains of at least ten more family members. The date is set. They will gather, just the six of them, on Sunday afternoon, January 6.

Now, it's time to tell Sheriff Pitts about Richard. They brace for it. It will not be easy. Luckily, Sheriff Pitts is the only one in the office when they arrive. Ree and James sit in the two chairs facing Sheriff Pitts and breathe in.

"I gather with you both here that there's something serious you need to tell me?" says the sheriff.

Ree looks at James. James looks at Ree. James speaks first. "Richard is dead, sheriff. I have his ashes."

Sheriff Pitts raises his eyebrows, waiting for more.

"We located a professor that Richard met after he left Lawrenceville. She currently lives in Asheville. She and Richard married and both taught at the University of North Carolina in Asheville. We recently visited her, and she told us Richard died of a heart attack last year," says Ree.

"We have his ashes," says James. "We feel telling you is the right thing to do."

"We know Uncle Richard's death solves nothing. We still don't know who killed Mother," says Ree. "We wanted you to know about Uncle Richard though. Like Dad said, we think it's the right thing to do."

Sheriff Pitts looks at the two of them. There's sadness in his eyes. "I know this whole experience has been horrible, especially for you, James. I don't know where we go from here. Will you have a funeral?"

"Yes, Sunday. But it's only for us—Aunt Maude, Gus, and Harold," says Ree, with blush creeping onto her face when she mentions Harold. Not everyone knows that they are an item.

"Just a quiet graveside memorial in the old historic cemetery," adds James.

"Go with God, and thank you for coming to me. I personally see no need to tell this story to the public. I think that's your call," says Sheriff Pitts.

"Thank you, Sheriff Pitts," says James, who stands and shakes the sheriff's hand.

"Yes, sheriff, thank you. You have always been fair with us," says Ree.

"I guess, in my own way, I am trying to make up for Sheriff Croft. I lay much of what you have gone through at his door," he says.

"You are an honorable man," says James.

A muscle moves in Sheriff Pitt's jaw, a sign he is touched by what James said.

\*\*\*

James, Virginia, Ree, and Harold have reservations at Hotel Button Gwinnett for early dinner. After they are seated inside the restaurant, Harold asks about Gus. He would normally be with them.

"Well, it seems Miss Gladys has given up on me. She and Gus have a date tonight," says James.

"Is that a look of relief on your face, James?" asks Harold.

James chuckles. "Maybe. I sure will miss those casseroles, though."

Ree laughs out loud. It's contagious. Soon they are all laughing.

After ordering, they discuss funeral arrangements for Richard, and they fill Harold in on the trip to Asheville and the later trip to see Sheriff Pitts.

Harold asks James, "Are you relieved, knowing about Richard's years after he left Lawrenceville?"

"Yes, and I am so happy about Richard having a full life with someone who loved him. The books he wrote and his teaching, too—I know he was in his element. I can't help but think about how hard it must have been though, living with the shadow of being accused of murder."

"Plus, he was robbed of time with us, and he would have loved watching Virginia grow up," says Ree.

Changing the subject, Harold says, "Before we order some of their famous pies—coconut, lemon meringue, pecan—I think we need to toast to the new year. There are many adventures ahead for all of us. I love a new year, keeping the good from last year and starting new."

"Hear, hear," says James, standing. They all follow suit and the four clink their glasses together.

"Here's to 1963," says Harold.

"Yes, to 1963," Ree and James echo in unison.

"And you, Virginia?" asks Ree.

"To 1963. But, when we leave, may I go to Bill's house to play Monopoly? His parents invited me." Virginia sits very straight, afraid of her mom's answer. She has waited until the last minute to ask.

"Yes, have fun. Bill's father called me a week ago to invite you."

Virginia breathes out. She has been holding her breath, waiting for her mom's answer. Good. She can see the new year in with Bill.

"Oh, I forgot to tell you. Gus has asked me over to his house later tonight. It seems Miss Gladys has a friend she wants me to meet," says James.

"Well, let's toast to that," says Harold. They clink glasses again.

"Sorry you two. I guess you'll have to see the new year in together, alone," smiles James.

Harold smiles at Ree. "I think we can manage that."

## Chapter Thirty-Five
*Sunday, January 6, 1963*

After Sunday dinner, James and Ree share the telephone in a call to Charlotte. Charlotte bemoans the fact that she will not be here for Richard's graveyard service. James repeatedly thanks her for sharing Richard's ashes with them.

Soon after, they drive to the cemetery, just the three of them—James, Ree, Virginia. Pulling into the old cemetery, they pass Mason's grave on the way to James' family plot. Virginia begins to cry at the solemnness of the situation and at the loss of a father she can barely remember.

Harold and Gus are waiting at the grave site when they arrive. The local gravedigger has come and gone. James has made sure everything is ready for the burial. They hear the crunching sound of Aunt Maude's tires on the winter leaves as she drives up. Any other time, James would find it amusing that Maude's car cost more than many people's houses here in Lawrenceville.

They stand around the gravesite. James clears his throat and begins. "We are not here today to remember the tragedy in Richard's life. We are here to honor the wonderful man we each knew as Richard—a brilliant man who followed our covenant with God more than any human I've ever known. He loved God and he loved others as himself."

Aunt Maude begins to cry. You can barely hear her soft moans over James's clear, strong voice.

"We are here today to count ourselves lucky to have had Richard in our lives," he continues. "Let's take a moment to quietly reflect on the place he holds in our individual hearts."

It's like the traffic has stopped on the highway, as if the birds have stopped singing. Suddenly no geese are flying overhead. Nothing moves. It's like the entire earth is remembering Richard, breathing quietly with honor and reverence.

"I would like to share…" says James, starting again.

"Wait. Listen," says Ree.

The crunch of tires on leaves. The family turns, and cars as far as the eye can see are turning into the old cemetery, one by one. They are coming to honor Richard.

"How in heaven's name?" asks James.

"I told Preacher Foster," says Gus. "I am sorry I went against your wishes. I thought the people of Lawrenceville would want to honor Richard, and it seems I was right."

Pure Gus. Always right.

In this case, Ree thinks, he is right. Richard deserves the honor.

Gus puts his arm around James' shoulder. "They want to support you… And Reeda… And Virginia," he says.

Reverend Foster is the first to reach the gravesite, soon followed by so many people. It seems the entire town of Lawrenceville has come.

"I hope you will allow us to help you bury Richard," says Reverend Foster approaching the family. Everyone is worried. James hasn't said a word. The reverend adds, "I have to say most of the people of Lawrenceville are here, including Miss Mamie Evers who can sing 'Amazing Grace' like no one I know. Would you like that, James?"

James nods his head, as Ree moves closer to him and takes his hand. Miss Evers moves to stand nearer to James and Ree. She sings "Amazing Grace" and when she reaches the third verse the entire group begins to sing with her:

> Through many dangers, toils, and snares,
> I have already come;
> 'tis grace hath brought me safe thus far,
> and grace will lead me home.

## Chapter Thirty-Six
*Monday, January 7, 1963*

Walking to her desk at the *News-Herald*, Ree sees a large stack of newspapers, all dated 1962. They are last year's papers that will be bound and archived along with the other books in the storage room. Another year put on the shelf.

Ree stops to leaf through the papers. John Glenn is the first American to orbit the earth. Rhodes Jordan was elected mayor of Lawrenceville. The Central Gwinnett boys won the state championship in Class A basketball. The Cuban Missile Crisis in October.

On a personal note, Virginia climbed the clock tower and found a boyfriend, Ree found Harold, the family found Charlotte and buried Richard. *1962. What a year.*

Thinking back to the service for Richard, Ree remembers how proud she was of James. While thanking the crowd for coming to memorialize Richard, James mentioned that Richard could never have killed Mildred. Someday, they would find out who did.

Ree has been lost in thought. She looks up to see Miss Betty walking across the newsroom. Miss Betty hands Ree a white envelope.

This was in the morning mail. It's probably from a member of your fan club or from someone with a hot news tip."

"Sure," says Ree, taking the envelope from Miss Betty.

"I, along with everyone I know, feel gratitude that you were able to find out about your Uncle Richard and were able to bring him home to rest," Miss Betty adds.

"Thank you. It's such a relief to find him. I love that he led a full life."

"I've never taken the courage to tell you, but I don't know a soul who thinks he murdered your mother."

"That means a lot to me. I'll pass it on to Father. Thank you, Miss Betty."

Miss Betty walks halfway across the news room and turns back. "Tell that handsome Harold hello from me."

Ree laughs out loud. Miss Betty never fails to bring up Ree's love life. She picks up the envelope with child-like printing and Ree's address at work. Just like the threatening note she received—the one that had been addressed to her home.

**You didn't listen. You should.**

**If you continue, I will kill your daughter.**

**Your choice.**

Ree crumples the note in her right hand, making a fist. She crushes the letter to make it disappear and holds back a scream. *Virginia. She can't let something happen to Virginia.*

Her first instinct is to run to Harold. Crushed letter in hand, she races through the newsroom, past Miss Betty, out the *News-Herald* building and down Perry Street. She needs to see Harold. She rushes up the stairs to his office to find him with a client.

Harold takes one look at Ree and motions with his head for Ree to wait in the empty conference room. Finally, Ree hears Harold tell his client goodbye. "Ree, what's the matter? Is it James?"

Ree hands the crushed note to Harold.

Harold smooths out the note and reads it. Taking Ree by the hand, Harold pulls her out the office door and locks the door behind him. "We are taking this straight to Sheriff Pitts. Come with me."

Ree follows Harold down the stairs and over to the sheriff's office. Harold enters the office first, calling for Sheriff Pitts, who emerges from a back room.

"Hello, Harold and Reeda. How may I help you? But first, please sit down," says the sheriff.

Harold takes the envelope out of his pocket as he and Reeda sit. He hands it to the sheriff.

Sheriff Pitts examines the envelope and frowns. Reading the contents, Sheriff Pitts says, "What is this about? Why would anyone threaten your daughter?"

Ree begins to cry.

Harold answers, "It is her mother's murder case. She is trying to solve it, and someone is afraid. By the way, this is the second letter she's received. Same strange printing on the front and threatening content in the letter."

Sheriff Pitts looks at the envelope again. Its child-like printing is eerie.

"May I keep this letter?" asks the sheriff.

"Yes, please," answers Ree.

"Reeda, you are to take this very seriously," says the sheriff.

"We are doing everything we can to protect her. Now we'll have to watch Virginia, too. James and I are making sure Ree is not out at night without one of us with her. Right, Ree?" says Harold.

Ree doesn't answer.

"Ree?"

No answer.

"Ree, you did show James the letter, didn't you?" Harold asks insistently once he realizes the reason for her silence.

"I didn't want to worry him." says Ree, softly.

Harold stands. "Sheriff, thank you for your time. Ree, come with me. We are going to see James. He needs to know."

Sheriff Pitts sits staring at the envelope long after Harold and Ree have left.

## Chapter Thirty-Seven
*Sunday, January 13, 1963*

Ree can't get the argument between Richard and her mother off her mind—the argument Dennis and Charlotte have both mentioned. Charlotte told them Richard and Mildred had an argument about some papers her mother had found at the Feely House. The least she can do is go to the Feely House and look around.

"Dad," Ree shouts into the house, "I'll be back soon. I'm going to the Feely House to look around."

James yells back, "Not without me. Give me a minute." James has hardly let Ree out of sight since she and Harold showed him the mysterious letters. Ree knows he's not sleeping well; she hears him getting up all through the night. She knows he has a pistol in his nightstand.

The Feely House. It is the most important house in Lawrenceville and sits next door to Ree and James. The house is named for Augustus Feely, originally from Denver. He was a wealthy businessman connected with the Seaboard Railway and lived in the stately home with his wife, Eugenia. Both of the Feely's died of influenza in December of 1932, and the house was opened as a historic landmark shortly thereafter.

 Walking into the historic home never disappoints, Ree thinks as she and James head toward the home situated next to them on the Lawrenceville Square. The house is stunning. It is a two-storied brick home framed by rising round columns The second floor has a balcony—it must have been lovely to sit there with a cup of tea and watch the goings-on around the square.

 Ree and James have the same key Mildred had used in her time as a docent for the Feely House. They never thought to return it. James and Ree enter the wide hall that runs from the front to the back of the house.

 The Feely Home is a four-over-four house—four large rooms downstairs topped with four rooms upstairs. The front parlor is to the right, the library is to the left.

 Ree remembers her mother standing in the library while she told visitors the history of the house. Ree and James start their search there.

 There are two tufted, navy-blue velvet, over-stuffed chairs in the room and a mahogany desk that belonged to Mr. Feely's father. Ree remembers her mother telling visitors the desk was brought over from France in the early 1800s.

James stands back to look over the shelves of books that line three walls "Nothing stands out. It would take months to go through every single book on these shelves," says James.

"Let's try the desk," says Ree. "It seems probable papers would be found in a desk."

No luck. The drawers of the desk are completely empty.

The two move to the parlor. After searching a leather-topped parlor table, they search an étagère, also called a whatnot holder. It is filled with intricate porcelain dolls. Again, no luck.

Ree and James move back to the library where Ree plops down in one of the navy-blue velvet chairs.

"This is like searching for a needle in a haystack," says James. "We don't even know the papers are still here. Mildred may have done something with them."

Ree rests her head on the back of the chair. She sighs, a sign she is frustrated. She closes her eyes for a moment and opens them. She is staring at a book on the shelf that is upside down. It is volume one of Gibbon's *The History of the Decline and Fall of the Roman Empire.*

"Dad, that book is upside down. The one on the Roman Empire. Can you reach it?"

James easily retrieves the book from the shelf and opens it. Several yellowed sheets of newsprint fall to the floor. James picks one up. The article is from *The Denver Post.* It is dated 1930.

The headline reads: *Daughter of Denver Councilman Arrested for Shoplifting.*

The article goes on to say Delia Futuro was arrested for stealing a diamond bracelet at the Denver Dry Department Store. The fact that her father was a councilman may have played a part in her being released with no charges filed. It seems there were other thefts that had been covered up.

The other articles basically say the same thing, except for one article. It's about the engagement of Delia Futuro to Louis Scott of Lawrenceville, Georgia. James passes them to Ree. She is stunned.

*Imagine mousy Delia stealing something. Could that have ruined Louis Scott's chances of being elected?*

"I remember Louis was running for the state senate the year Mildred was murdered," says James. "All those obnoxious campaign slogans. That was 1934. This article about the engagement indicates a November 1932 wedding. Ree, did the senator know about the thefts?"

The sentence hangs in the air for a while.

"Dad," Ree asks, "Do you think Senator Scott killed Mother? Could he have killed her over what she knew, over what these articles say?"

"I just don't know, Reeda. But I know we need to call the sheriff." James gathers the articles. "Let's take these home. We'll call from there."

\* \* \*

James and Ree are ready for bed when the telephone rings. Ree rushes to answer and finds the sheriff on the line.

"I apologize for calling so late, but I knew you and James would want to know about my visit to the Scott's."

Ree feels her heart beating faster. James walks over to stand close by Ree. She shares the phone with him. "Yes, sheriff. Dad and I are both here. Go ahead," she says.

"Senator Scott said he didn't know about the thefts, but it was obvious he was lying. He was so fidgety the entire time we talked. He would not make eye contact with me—always looking up when I asked about the thefts. Delia admitted to the thefts. According to her, she was terrified someone in Lawrenceville would find out and ruin Louis' chance to be elected. She is still terrified someone will find out. It would damage her husband."

"What will you do?" asks Ree.

"Absolutely nothing. The statute of limitations has long run out. I plan to keep this information to myself. I can't tell you what to do, but I would be pleased if you did the same."

James interjects, "But what about Ree and my granddaughter? They have been threatened. If the Scotts are involved in those threats, I will not be quiet."

"I understand that," says the sheriff. "Please let me do a little digging before you make this public."

"Don't take too much time, Sheriff Pitts."

"No, I assure you, I won't. Try to sleep tonight, James. We'll see what tomorrow brings."

Ree hangs up the phone and looks at James. She doubts either of them will sleep tonight.

## Chapter Thirty-Eight
*Monday, January 14, 1963*

After the predictably sleepless night, James and Ree are having coffee in the kitchen. They review the events of yesterday.

"The Feely's were originally from Denver. I think we can assume the articles were mailed to them by a Denver relative," says James.

"That makes…" says Ree. She is interrupted by the telephone ringing. Probably not good news at seven o'clock on a Monday morning. She answers.

"Reeda, Mr. Monroe here. Delia Scott is dead. Rumor has it, it's suicide. I'm thinking we need to put out a Tuesday paper. Can you come in early?"

Ree puts her hand over the phone and tells James that Delia is dead. She can hear Mr. Monroe even though her hand still covers the phone, "Reeda. Reeda, are you there?"

"I'm here, Mr. Monroe. I'll come in right away."

"Can you try to track down Sheriff Pitts before you come in?"

"Yes," answers Ree.

It pops in Ree's head that she may be writing an article about the wife of her mother's killer. She downs her coffee and rushes to get dressed. James is waiting for her when she comes downstairs.

"Please tell me what is going on. Delia Scott is dead?" says James.

"Yes. Mr. Monroe says rumor has it she committed suicide. He wants to put out a paper tomorrow and wants me working right away."

"Please keep me posted. You know I worry."

At that moment, the doorbell rings.

"Good grief," says Ree.

"I'll get it," says James. James opens the door to Sheriff Pitts.

"Good morning, James. Reeda. I thought you should be the first to know. Delia Scott is dead."

Ree smiles. "You're late, sheriff. Half the town must know. Mr. Monroe wants me at work. He wants to put a special edition of the paper out tomorrow. As a matter of fact, I am supposed to be tracking you down right now."

"Dadgummit. There are no secrets in this town," says the sheriff.

"Come to the kitchen. I'll brew a fresh pot of coffee, and we can hear all your news," says James.

"Senator Scott called me at five o'clock this morning," says Sheriff Pitts. He got up during the night and Delia was not in their bed. After searching for her, he found her in the observatory on a sofa. There was a note. She couldn't live with the fear of exposure. That's all the note said."

"Odd she would kill herself over a charge of shoplifting in her early years," says James.

"I thought the same thing," says the sheriff. "It doesn't make sense."

"For my article, how did she commit suicide?" says Ree.

"Pills. An overdose. The bottle was on the sofa with her."

"That's okay for publication?"

"Yes. Now, I have got to get going. I'll touch base with you later."

"Thank you for coming to see us, sheriff," says James. "Good luck in sorting this out."

## Chapter Thirty-Nine
*Tuesday, January 15, 1963*

Ree and James are on the way to the sheriff's office. Sheriff Pitts called James after lunch and asked that they come to his office. The two are stopped multiple times on their way.

"What do you think about the senator's wife committing suicide?"

"Was she ill, like did she have cancer or something?"

"Did the senator kill her?"

James responded to most of the questions.

"I don't know what to think."

"I don't know if his wife had cancer."

"I don't think the senator killed her."

Relieved to be off the street and away from the swirl of rumors, James and Ree sit down at the sheriff's request.

"James, Ree. Buckle up. I have news about Mildred's murder."

"The senator killed her?" says Ree.

The sheriff hesitates, then responds. "No, his wife did."

Ree's eyes widen, but James is the one to respond. "Are you sure?"

"Yes, the senator told me she did. Mrs. Scott overheard an argument between your wife and Richard. Your wife found some newspaper articles sent from Denver to the Feelys concerning Mrs. Scott. Mrs. Scott grew up in Denver, and it seems she was guilty of several instances of shoplifting before she married the senator. This could have hurt the senator's chances of being elected, of course. I think he was running for office at that time. Richard wanted Mildred to take the letters to the sheriff, but Mildred refused."

"My mother protected the senator? Saved his reputation?" says Ree.

"It seems those were her intentions, but Mrs. Scott did not trust her. The senator said Mrs. Scott told him she committed the murder for him."

"Good grief," says Ree.

"What happens now?" asks James.

"If Mrs. Scott were alive, she would be charged with malice murder. She intentionally killed another person with a malicious state of mind. That's the definition of malice murder, and the charge fits Mrs. Scott."

"What about the senator?" asks Ree.

"He is not an accessory to murder. He wasn't present and didn't even know about his wife's involvement until after the fact. But hold on. There's more."

The sheriff gets up and walks around his desk, gathering his thoughts. He sits down. He composes himself and says, "The senator sent the notes to you, Reeda."

James' face turns red. He's furious. "That little pompous ass. Threatening my family. I'll…."

"Please tell me there will be consequences," says Ree.

"First, he'll be arraigned. Then, yes, he'll stand trial, probably as a felon. He prizes his reputation so much. It's destroyed. He's lost his wife. I wonder if his sentencing will matter much to him," says the sheriff.

"Oh, yes it will. If he gets a light sentence, he'll just move away and start over," says James. He stands up to leave. He's heard enough. James gathers himself, shakes the sheriff's hand, and thanks him for being so forthcoming with them.

"It's going to take me some time to process all this," Ree says. "But it is rewarding to finally have a resolution, to know what happened. I have to confess, I always suspected Dennis Forrester. He is such a strange person. I think my mother saw another Dennis behind the strangeness, and she liked him. Of course, Dennis loved her. I am going to try to remember that people like the Scotts are in the minority. We are supposed to forgive. Is that possible, sheriff?"

"I work on that myself, Reeda." The sheriff opens his office door for them. "You two take care."

## Chapter Forty
*Thursday, January 17, 1963*

Ree and Mr. Monroe are discussing the world in general in his office at the *News-Herald*.

"There's an article in last week's paper that suggests our Gwinnett population is going to double by 1983. In the next twenty years, we'll grow from 48,000 persons to 86,000. Big changes coming our way," says Ree.

"Yes. Big changes. Three days ago, Alabama elected George Wallace as its governor. You know, he actually said *Segregation now, segregation tomorrow, and segregation forever!* in his inaugural speech. Despite Wallace's speech, I predict 1963 is going to bring changes, and I think those changes are long overdue," says Mr. Monroe.

"I couldn't agree more, Mr. Monroe. I see a Lawrenceville in the future with no restrictions about where anyone eats, lives, works, or goes to school. That's my vision," says Ree.

"I share that vision with you, Reeda. I believe it will happen in our lifetimes. Now, locally, I have a story for you to write. It's about Gus."

"Gus Montgomery? What on earth has he done?"

"He is receiving a community service award tonight at the Central Gwinnett PTA meeting. The meeting begins at seven o'clock. Can you cover it?"

"Oh, I wouldn't miss it," says Ree, grinning.

\* \* \*

Harold drives Ree home after the PTA meeting at the high school. He puts an arm around Ree's shoulders to bring her closer to him. "I am so proud of you," says Harold.

Ree's eyes widen. "Whatever for?" says Ree.

"I know in my heart you are going to write a story about Gus that puts him on a pedestal."

"No, but I will write about all he has given to Lawrenceville in the past and all he is currently giving. He deserves this article, Harold."

"Yes, he does. But back to being proud of you. You solved the mystery of your mother's death. That is huge. And you are raising a phenomenal daughter, Ree, regardless of your insecurities. And, *most* important to me, you have fallen in love with me."

"You think so?"

"I hope so. You know I love you. I will do anything for you, Reeda Jones."

"Good," says Ree. "I have to complete Aunt Clarisse's last wishes and spread her ashes at one last location. Remember, that's what I requested as a Christmas gift from you."

"My gosh, where this time?" says Harold.

"Paris," says Ree.

Harold slows down. "Paris?" says Harold.

"Yes, Paris," says Ree.

Harold looks at Ree. *What will she say? Will she think I'm rushing things. Oh, Harold, just see what she says.* Harold clears his throat. "Okay, we'll go to Paris to spread Aunt Clarisse's ashes, but only after you do one thing for me," he says.

"What's that?" says Ree.

"Marry me."

## Acknowledgements

IT HAS BEEN AN UTTER JOY to write a novel set in a town I love, the town I have called home for eleven years.

I have so much gratitude for Ruth Braselton Morris and Vicki McGee Walden who grew up in Lawrenceville and remember it as it was in 1962. Ruth labeled every store existing on Lawrenceville Square at the time on paper, and she and Vicki walked the square with me, pointing out where everything was in the sixties. The two of them told me about the school system, the social life, and the people of Lawrenceville at the time. A huge thank you to Ruth and Vicki. I really think they took this journey with me.

The following Lawrenceville natives also provided valuable input and confirmation of Ruth's and Vicki's information: Marilyn Thompson Parks, Patsy Craft Price, Rev. Dr. Hoyt Huff, Jr., Kay Smith Payne, Patricia Oakes Taylor, Sanford Thompson, Van Britt, Frankie Dowis Britt, and Margaret Holt Mathis. Thank you for sharing your memories of Lawrenceville in the early 1960s.

What a lucky author I am. Dawn Richerson has been involved in the editing and publishing of all my books, including this fifth book, *The December Postcards*. I always say my books would not have seen the light of day without her. It's true.

The ladies at the Gwinnett Historical Society were a huge help. They are Beverly Paff, Francis Johnson, and Peggie Johnson.

## The December Postcards

I spent many days there hovering over the microfiche reader reading the news of Lawrenceville during October, November, and December of 1962. Thanks to Beverly, I finally learned to use the microfiche reader.

Actual newspaper articles, such as the dedication of a bridge to Marvin Allison, the story of the mayoral race, the Central Gwinnett Band story, the article by Bruce Still and Betty Cole, and others, mentioned in this novel are news stories that came from the *Lawrenceville News-Herald* editions from October 1962 through January 1963.

My sister-in-law, Sharron Smith, shared her experiences as a reporter for a small-town paper. Her experiences were invaluable. Thank you to her and to husband, Gene, for the support they always give me.

I spent an enjoyable hour or so in Mayor David Still's office learning about his memories of Lawrenceville. I so appreciate his time and his love of Lawrenceville.

Julia Webb Davis, whose mother, Marion Allison Webb, was owner of the *News-Herald*, provided me with information about the interior of the *News-Herald* in 1962.

Judy Stegall and Crystal Pinsky helped with me see the Methodist church as it was then. Judy shared her wedding pictures, so I could have a visual of the inside of the Methodist church.

L.C. Smith and Becky Lester remembered you could buy records and books at Rich's in downtown Atlanta. You wouldn't believe the lack of bookstores in the Lawrenceville area in the early sixties.

Nona and J.M. Patterson were teaching at Central Gwinnett High School during the time period when *The December Postcards* is set. I thank them for sharing their memories over Mexican food. And the same for Marie and Bob Beiser. It was wonderful to have lunch with them and listen to their stories of Lawrenceville. They were living in Lawrenceville and teaching in the Gwinnett County Public School System in 1962.

My brother, Jerry Jones, introduced me to Soviet Naval Officer Vasili Arkhipov, the flotilla commander of four nuclear-armed submarines headed for Cuba in October 1962. He is mentioned briefly in chapter twenty-five. Arkhipov wisely prevented the launching of a nuclear warhead against the USS Randolph. The BBC produced a documentary entitled "Missile Crisis: The Man Who Saved the World" about Arkhipov. His story is fascinating, and I encourage you to research him.

Ruth Braselton Morris and Vicki McGee Walden were beta readers for *The December Postcards*, as was Donna Hill, long-time friend and reader of one hundred books a year. Thank you for catching any errors made in the telling of the story.

What can I say about the talented, beautiful Susan Sikes Davis? I am so grateful to her. She hosted a book launch for three of my five books in her fabulous Lawrenceville shop, Sikes and Davis. Susan even dressed as Ole Luella and passed out predictions for guest's lives. She has supported my books in so many ways, and I am more than thankful for her.

Thank you to my son, Dr. Jeff Smith, for discussing the legal consequences of Senator Scott's threatening letters to Ree with me.

I am a blessed lady. I have beautiful friends in my life. They lift me up. They add joy to my life. Thank you for your love and support.

I am so lucky to walk this life with my husband of sixty plus years, L.C. Smith. He continues to support me in ways too numerous to count and never says, "Oh, no. You are writing another book?" Love and gratitude, L.C.

I am thankful to be a part of the Jones and Smith families. Yes, I was a Jones and married a Smith. And I am thankful for our wonderful children—Doug, Christy, Jeff, and Katie.

## About the Author

ALAYNE SMITH is a retired broadcast journalism teacher who earned M. Ed. and Ed. S. degrees in Instructional Technology from the University of Georgia. She taught for over twenty-five years in Gwinnett County, Ga., where she developed the first broadcast journalism course at the high school level. With other Gwinnett County broadcast journalism teachers, she contributed to the development of an eight-course continuum of courses in broadcast journalism and video production. She was Bell South Teacher of the Year and, in 2003, was Brookwood High School's Teacher of the Year. She served as a committee member for the International Student Media Festival from 1995 to 1998 and as a CNN Student Bureau Advisor, from 1999 to 2001.

*Ellen and the Three Predictions,* published in March 2017 by Cactus Moon Publications, is a historical fiction novel written for young adults and Alayne's first novel. Set in the late 1950s and early 1960s, *Ellen and the Three Predictions* details the life of an aspiring broadcast journalist, Ellen Jones, and the predictions made for Ellen's life by Old Luella, a local soothsayer.

*Educating Sadie,* published in August 2019, was a finalist in the 2018 William Faulkner–William Wisdom Creative Writing Competition. *Educating Sadie* follows one woman's struggle to help another woman rise above a life of poverty and abuse in nineteenth-century Alabama. Amanda Oglesby is a first-year teacher who meets Sadie, a sharecropper's wife, on the night of the first open house at her new school. Childless, Sadie is drawn to the school. She is bright and eager to learn. The relationship develops when Amanda invites Sadie to attend daily classes at the school. A benevolent school board chairman, a beloved boarding house owner, a midwife, a handsome plantation owner, and a misanthrope move in the background of *Educating Sadie,* a portrait of the American South at the turn of the century.

Alayne's third novel, *This Is Ellen Jones Reporting,* follows the story of Ellen Jones as she follows her dream of becoming a broadcast journalist. Set in 1961, this sequel to *Ellen and the Three Predictions* draws on the developing stories of Luke and Ellen with glimpses of her beloved Callander and college life as they pursue their degrees. Again, Cuba is a thread in Smith's novels as Zia works on a documentary about the real events at the Bay of Pigs and Ellen competes for a Peabody Award with her story of a former literature teacher at the University of Havana who was forced to leave the Cuba he loves.

*A Mystery Solved, A Prediction Fulfilled* is a dual-timeline novel that opens in 1962 with college junior Ellen Jones, who has decisions to make about her career and personal life. Does she have feelings for Jo Jo, the boy who grew up with her at Callander? But her most pressing current dilemma is a mystery back in her hometown of Marshall, Alabama. A carving in a mint julep cabinet indicates her great grandmother married one man in May 1866, while an inscription in the family Bible says she married someone else. This Ellen Jones novel is the third and last in the series.

Alayne is a member of the Atlanta Writers Club, the Georgia Association for Instructional Technology, the Georgia Writers Association, the Southeastern Writers Association, and the Society of Children's Book Writers and Illustrators. She currently lives in Lawrenceville, Georgia, with her husband and a wonderful cat named Ellen. Learn more about Alayne at her website, https://alaynesmith.com.

Made in the USA
Columbia, SC
02 October 2024